Burning Djinn of Fire

Grimoires of a Middle-aged Witch Universe

Destiny of a Middle-aged Witch
Book 1

Renee George

Barkside of the Moon Press

Burning Djinn of Fire

Grimoires of a Middle-aged Witch Universe

Destiny of a Middle-aged Witch Book 1

Copyright © 2024 by Renee George

Print Publication March 28, 2024

Print ISBN: 978-1-947177-50-5

Publisher: Barkside of the Moon Press

For my husband and son,
Steve and Taylor
I love you both heart and soul.

Acknowledgments

I have to thank the usual people for helping me get to the end of this book.

First, Robbin Clubb, Robyn Peterman, and Michele Vail, my critique partners, know just when to kick my ass when I need it!

Second, to the readers and my Rebels, without you all, what would be the point? I am so happy and blessed to have you guys in my corner!

Third, but not least, coffee. Thank you, strong black coffee, for giving me the energy to bring this baby home. You are the miracle in my life.

Seven months ago, goddess magic allowed me, the very human Marigold Everlee, to have a couple of sizzling nights with the very paranormal Zev. He was tall, dark, and smoking hot.

Literally. He's an ifrit--a fire-magic-wielding djinn.

Spoiler alert: When the goddess magic poofed---so did Zev.

Yeah. I was ghosted after he promised me, he'd be back. His disappearance turned my heart to ash. But you know what? I'm middle-aged and marvelous, baby. Crying over spilled magic isn't going to change what happened to my one-sided love connection.

I have new aspirations: being the best bad-ass witch possible. My new bestie is teaching me the ways of eclectic magic, and I'm throwing all my energy into the process. I've always been a little hippy-dippy, so using my crystals and herbs for spell work should come naturally to me, right?

Wrong.

Just when I think I'm getting the hang of potions, a fire spell blows up in my face, leaving a cryptic message scorched into my kitchen ceiling.

From Zev. *What the what!?*

It seems Zev didn't want to disappear after all.

I may be a magical mess, but no one gets away with hurting the people I love, including my stubborn, sarcastic, sexy genie.

Watch out, world. This girl is on fire. Get out of the way ... or get burned.

Chapter One

The acrid stench of the giant, horrid beast turned my stomach. With a name like snotgurgle, I knew it would be disgusting, but I hadn't been prepared for how much nauseating mucus would be covering the creature. It resembled a colossal green booger. So freaking gross.

"Oh, holy monstrosity." I swallowed as the sour taste of bile filled my mouth. I watched Zev, an annoyingly charming and unholy handsome fire djinn, run across the expansive field with the snotgurgle hot on his heels.

My heart skipped a beat. I wanted to yell at him to get his ifrit ass moving, but obviously, he was booking as fast as he could.

I hadn't seen him since the pixie mating frenzy until today, but man, I thought about him a lot. He'd shown up at the Iron Grove earlier that day. Keir had called him to act as Iris's fire guardian for her witch trial.

It was as bad as it sounded.

As the beast closed in on Zev, I staggered forward.

"Don't expose yourself, Marigold," Carver Martin, an eclectic witch I'd only met hours earlier, warned as he tugged me down, shielding me with the stone barrier outside the hedge maze behind the Iron Grove. "You don't want him catching your scent. Snotgurgles are relentless once they start hunting. Besides, you get slimed, you get dead."

Carver's father, Thomas, the witch of Archdruid Freya, had assigned Carver the task of babysitting me. Honestly, I thought it was Thomas' way of keeping both of us out of harm. A part of me felt like I was responsible for what was happening. My sister's boyfriend and magical mentor, Keir, had asked me to bring Iris her grimoires, and I'd asked Linda the Gnome to come along for the ride.

How in the hell could I have known that gnomes were a delicacy for Snotgurgles? Oh, and guess what else? Snotgurgles were nasty trolls that took great delight in torturing their food before eating it. I hoped like hell it hadn't eaten Linda.

I'd never forgive myself.

My anxiety level ramped up to ten as I gnawed on my thumbnail. Ugh. I'd already chewed all my fingernails until they bled. I dropped my hand and turned my gaze to Carver. "We can't hide. We have to help."

"How do you suggest we help?" Carver asked. His unnaturally black hair had fallen over his bushy brows and into his eyes. He brushed it back. "The druids and their tru-craft witches will struggle to take that creature down. This kind of troll is immune to magic and most physical attacks. His mucous is poisonous, and the snot from its nose can dissolve flesh and bone. You go out there, and they'll have to worry about protecting you while trying to do an already impossible job."

"Fine," I conceded. Carver and his stupid logic. "I can't believe creatures like this exist." It was a sentiment I'd repeated to myself often since finding out my sister Iris was a tru-craft witch.

"I wish the snotgurgle was the worst thing I've ever seen," Carver muttered.

I didn't have the emotional capacity to think about what could be worse. My fears were for the people I loved. "What about my sister?" I craned my neck again to see if I could spot her on the field. Zev had come out of the woods with the monster, but I hadn't seen Iris. "Where is she?"

Carver put his hand on my shoulder and gave it a gentle squeeze. "Iris is strong, and so is Keir. Keep the faith."

Easier said than done. I'd never been religious, but I'd always been drawn to the spirituality of the natural world, so I prayed to anyone who might be listening to keep my sister and Keir safe. And Zev, too.

The archdruids and their witches lined up on the grassy field like a small army, ready to do battle against the monstrous abomination.

"I hope you're right." I couldn't cower away. People I cared about—that I loved—were in danger, and I'd never been one to sit on the sidelines. Hell, I was usually the person starting the fight. Hiding behind a wall wasn't my jam.

I moved again for a better look, shrugging Carver's hand off when he attempted to stop me.

The snotgurgle, less than impressed by his newfound foes, undulated his gelatinous body in a horrifying dance. His gyrating bulbous hips shot fluorescent green globs of slime that sprayed over the grass and foliage.

I blinked. "Is that grass turning black?" The area around the snotgurgle had turned into a giant inky shadow surrounding the creature.

"Everything the slime touches dies," Carver said. "If I could find a vessel to collect some, I could formulate a spell or potion to neutralize the effects."

I whipped my gaze to him. "Can you do that now?"

He shook his head solemnly. "No. It would take hours, maybe days, to craft the right combination." His fists clenched as he rubbed his knuckles against the side of his black jeans. "I hate being sidelined."

I arched my brow. He'd argued with me about following the archdruids to the field, but I wondered if it was an argument he'd had no intention of winning. "You're worried, too. About your dad?"

"Thomas isn't my dad," he said without anger or malice. "He's my friend. And yes, I'm worried about him."

Biologically, Thomas was his father, but like me, Carver had been adopted as a baby and raised by parents who had loved him well. My dad was my dad, and no amount of genetics or lack thereof would change that fact. The same seemed to be true for Carver.

I nodded. "Thomas is powerful, too, and from what Iris has said, he's fought and survived other battles. They'll win," I told him with far more confidence than I felt. "They have to." I gasped, my relief palpable, when my sister Iris and Keir burst out of the forest at a full sprint. "Oh, thank everything good and chocolatey," I whispered.

Keir raced ahead of Iris, both of them looking as if they'd been run through the spin cycle before coming to an abrupt halt. The snotgurgle was caught between them and the archdruids.

Freya stood with Thomas and the others, each with a man or a woman by their side, hands joined.

"Power of air," I heard Thomas call out. "I bind thee to mine and thine, my kin to call and summon. Obey my will."

"Power of fire," a tall brunette with straight dark hair said, "I bind thee to mine and thine, my kin to call and summon. Obey my will."

A curvy woman wearing a bright red rockabilly dress covered in white polka dots shouted, "Power of earth. I bind thee to mine and thine, my kin to call and summon. Obey my will."

"Why isn't anything happening?" I demanded of Carver.

"Just wait," he answered without looking at me. His eyes were glued to the action... or rather lack thereof. "They're not done."

A petite blonde in a long white maxi dress voiced clearly, "Power of water, I bind thee to mine and thine, my kin to call and summon. Obey my will."

That was four elements from four out of the six druid groves.

Another woman with dark hair intoned, "Power of Air, I bind thee to mine and thine, my kin to call and summon. Obey my will."

That left only the Bezoar Grove to join in, and I wondered if Mathias Easton, the Ichabod Crane-looking leader of the grove, would allow old scars to see this assault on Iron Grove as an opportunity.

Easton's coven leader, a guy who was just as skinny and tall as he was, hesitated only a moment before adding his own command, "Power of Fire, I bind thee to mine and thine, my kin to call and summon. Obey my will."

Why wasn't anything happening? The snotgurgle had stopped his death dance and scratched his head as he stared at the group of druids and witches.

A sonic boom struck the center of the field. Carver and I were slammed to the ground. I scrambled to my feet to watch the horror unfold as glowing mucus exploded from the snotgurgle, followed by shouts of alarm.

The giant troll roared as it threw back his head and

sneezed, sending the largest loogie I've ever seen toward Archdruid Freya. Carver lurched forward, and then I watched helplessly as Zev jumped in front of Freya to take the hit.

A scream of anguish ripped my throat as I watched him crumple to the ground. "Zev!" Without thinking, I hiked up my skirt and sprinted toward the fallen ifrit.

I heard other roars, shouts, and screams, but I couldn't focus on them. I had to get to Zev. He hadn't moved since the rotting slime had hit him in the chest.

Let him be alive, I prayed. Don't let him die. I'd been flirting with the fiery ifrit for only a couple of months, but as the possibility of losing him forever loomed, I realized that my feelings for him went beyond a crush. He was a creature of fire, and I was a human. We couldn't be together. He'd told me that from the start, but the reality hadn't stopped my heart from opening and letting him in.

People were going down around me, but I was almost there. Twenty more yards. I can make it, I told myself. I high-stepped around several piles of goo. I was almost there!

I heard Iris's voice shouting above the fray, but I couldn't worry about what she was doing. Zev had risked his life to save everyone, and no one was trying to save him.

"Zev," I yelled as I slid to a halt and dropped to the ground beside him. The slime had burned through his leather jacket and was eating a hole into his chest. Flames swirled inside the wounds.

He turned to look at me, his eyes wide and his face a picture of pain. "No, *libbu ša*, you cannot be here," he managed to say. "Run, my beautiful love. Run."

"No," I told him. "I'm not leaving without you." I grabbed his arm to drag him away from the fight, and the skin on my hands and arms began to blister.

He yanked his body away, muttering in a language I couldn't understand, but it didn't stop me from getting the gist. He didn't want me to touch him. "I can't control the fire," he said. "You can't help me. You must go.'

Scalding tears burned my eyes. "I won't. I won't leave you."

A burst of colorful lights lit the night sky. I glanced away from Zev to see my sister floating in the air. Numbly, I asked, "What is she doing?"

My question was sort of answered when she bellowed, "I am Macha, earth mother and destroyer of men. You will come to heel!"

Who in the world was Macha? Had everyone lost their damned minds? Witches and most of the druids dropped to the ground as her light washed over the battlefield. The snotgurgle bellowed, beating his chest. His slimy coating grew even thicker over his skin.

My sister chanted some jibber-jabber words that I didn't understand. "Addlebyörn Bulbusbilgerbiersven of Höga Kusten."

But the troll responded with his own string of garbled words. "Du vet mitt namn?"

It shot a hot glob at her, and I shuddered as she

swiped it away as if she were shooing a fly. "You cannot defeat me, creature," she told it. "I am your undoing."

I felt a cold slap of putrid droplets as the snotgurgle shook his body like a dog after a bath. Searing pain burrowed into my side, and the left side of my face felt as if it were on fire. I looked down at Zev, my mouth open to scream, but I couldn't breathe, let alone make a sound.

"Marigold," he rasped.

"Iris!" someone near me yelled.

I collapsed to the ground, sucking to take in air. It must've taken all his will, and maybe some magic, but Zev managed to crawl to me. He wrapped me in his arms, his heated embrace a welcome respite to the cold chill consuming me. Flaming tears rolled down his cheeks as he cradled me in his lap.

"Don't try to move," he said when I reached up to touch his face. "Save your strength."

I mouthed, "We are together."

His eyes burned blue with the brightest flame. "Hush, my darling."

"We can't save what she is," I heard Iris say, but her voice sounded different. "There is a cost...."

Was Zev getting less hot, or was death finally taking me?

"We're losing her!" Keir shouted. "Iris! The rot is making it impossible to heal her. We can't stop it. Every time Zev tries, it takes more from her and more from him. It's like it's feeding on the magic, and they're both dying."

"I will fix the woman, as you say, Iris Everlee," Iris

said. "Olwen, who faced thirteen harrowing trials to win the heart of her love, your line runs true in this one. She is strong, a warrior's heart." Her hands glowed as she touched my forehead. "Transform, daughter," she commanded. "Transform and live."

I drew in a welcome breath as the agony disappeared. I could feel my muscles and bones shifting beneath my skin, and I blinked at Zev.

He let out a heaving sigh and then let me go as he fell over. Whatever was happening in my body made it impossible to move, speak, or help.

I tensed as Iris touched Zev's face. "Your time is not over, Za'fir of Mesopotamia. This is just the first trial on your path to love." Her hand glowed again and Zev's entire body bathed in her light. "Transform and live. Live to fulfill your path."

I let out a sob as Zev's cavernous chest wound knitted together, and his eyes opened. Flames shot out of his mouth and into the sky. When the stream of fire subsided, he collapsed back and passed out.

"Marigold," I heard Iris say as the world turned blissfully floaty. "What's wrong with her?"

"It's probably a side effect of Macha's magic," Keir replied. "She'll be okay. Zev, too."

*****

As I awakened, my head swam with momentary confusion, and then I remembered. Zev had cried as he'd held me in his arms. He'd been in rough shape—we both

10

had—but Iris had healed us. I squinted as I opened my eyes. "Zev?"

"I am here." His rich amber-brown eyes were framed by thick, dark lashes as his gaze met mine.

I was lying on a narrow mattress, and the small area around us was encircled by a white curtain. "Where are we?"

"The ballroom has been turned into a medical ward," he replied.

I frowned. There was something different about him. It wasn't the lustrous dark brown hair full of loose curls that made you want to run your fingers through them or his olive-tone skin, high cheekbones, and sharp jawline that made me want to take up sculpting.

"Zev," I said, my voice barely above a whisper as I studied him, the familiar leather jacket draped over his shoulder as he stood there.

"Marigold," he replied, his voice a low, rumbling murmur that sent a jolt of electricity coursing through me. "I feared I'd lost you forever."

I reached out, my fingers trembling as they brushed against his hand, feeling the warmth of his skin beneath my touch. Only, he was less warm than usual. Strange.

"Zev," I murmured, my heart pounding in my chest. "Are you ... are you okay? Why in the world did you jump in front of that nuclear snot rocket?"

"I owed Freya," he replied. With his other hand, he turned a flat circular stone across his knuckles like a coin. He flipped his hand over, and the stone was nestled in his hand. "My debt has been paid." He pressed the stone into my palm. It was smooth, shiny, and black with red veins. Etched in the top were a series of pointy triangles going in many directions.

"What's this?"

"It's *sebtusiptu*." Zev smiled. "A token."

The stone felt warm against my skin, and the longer I held it, the warmer it got. "A token for what?"

His brow raised as his smile turned sly. He closed my fingers around the token until my hand was a fist, and then he raised my knuckles to his lips and kissed them.

I shivered at the brush of his mouth against my skin. "A token of my esteem."

An unholy, schoolgirl giggle tittered from my lips. Ugh. How embarrassing.

His eyes, that's what was different. "Where are your flames?"

"They're no more," he answered quietly. "The goddess Macha has removed my fire."

I tried to punch down the hope surging inside me. "For good?" I sat up and slung my legs over the side of the gurney. Without his flames, we could be together. Was it really possible?

"For now," he replied.

My legs felt strange as they dangled off the edge, like they weren't my own. Then I stood up. My brow furrowed. "Did taking your fire make you shorter?" I was a tall woman at five-eight, but Zev had been a few inches taller than me. Now, I towered over him.

The corners of his mouth tugged into a smile. "You have also been changed by Macha."

There was a mirror on the wall behind him. I studied my reflection. My straight, dark brown, almost black hair hung loose around my shoulders. My skin had the same kiss of honey that it always did, and my brown eyes hadn't changed colors. Iris used to tell me that I looked like Catherine Zeta-Jones. Other than our coloring, I didn't really see it. "How have I been changed?"

Zev chuckled. "You've grown five inches for one."

"No." I shook my head and scoffed. "That's not a real thing." I looked at my hands. "Where are my rings?"

He gestured to a small side table. A chewed-up mess of metal and stones that vaguely resembled my rings littered a metal tray.

My eyes went wide. "What the hell happened to my jewelry?"

"You grew too big for them. The metal was cutting off the blood supply. It was the rings or your fingers."

My eyes narrowed to slits. "Are you saying I have fat fingers?"

"You have lovely, long fingers, *Libbu ša*, and I would drip them in jewels if that were your wish."

"So, you're granting wishes now, huh? I thought you said genies didn't do that kind of thing."

"I would make an exception for you, my beautiful flower." His dark gaze met mine, and I shivered. "For you, I would grant your every heart's desire."

"Oh, darling, I have a whole laundry list of requests," I smirked. "The first one involves you getting naked."

His grin grew wide. "Naked?"

"In the extreme," I said.

I laughed when he instantly dropped his jacket onto the floor. I set the stone down, and Zev paused his strip-tease. He picked up the stone and put it with my rings. "This is yours now. Keep it close to you."

I gave him a crooked smile. "As a token of your esteem."

"So a part of me will always be with you."

*****

A part of me will always be with you.... Zev's words lingered in my head as I looked around the room, orienting myself back to the present. The walls were covered in macrame art, boho chic straw plates and jars of crystals littering the freestanding shelves. In other words, I was in my own bedroom and no longer at Iron Grove with the fireless ifrit who had metaphorically scorched my panties off.

Even though it had been seven months ago, it felt like yesterday.

I sat up and stretched my back. "Big day," I reminded myself as I picked up Zev's token from the selenite bowl on my nightstand. Holding on to a rock from an ex-lover was silly, but it was tangible evidence that our relation-ship had been real. It had meant something, and I wasn't ready to give it up. I'd laid my clothes out the night before. A chocolate-tiered maxi skirt with pockets, a yellow and blue floral peasant blouse, and a tan bra and panty set that I loved so much I'd bought them in all the colors. I grabbed up the garments and trekked down the hall to the bathroom.

Carver and the boys would be here soon for our magic lessons and to help me stir a complicated potion— with a few modifications I'd read about on an internet forum for witches. Should I tell him? Probably. Would he try to stop me? Definitely. Which meant I wasn't going to loop him in.

I'd lost Zev, and I worried I'd never get him back.

Not if I didn't take matters into my own hands.

Chapter Two

My kitchen brought me a sense of solace. It was painted sage green with accents of mustard yellow, terra-cotta, peach, and turquoise. Artisanal ceramics, vintage glassware, and decorative woven baskets added vibrancy.

Macramé planters and hanging racks of dried herbs on my windowsills helped to bring a bit of nature into the house. The morning sun twinkled through pendants of hanging crystals, twinkling like string lights, and transformed my kitchen into a magical haven—perfect for spell work.

"Double, bubble, toil, and yuck, so terrible." I stirred the stinky potion on my gas range that I'd been brewing for the past hour and made a face as I turned to the second page of the *Grimorium Magnus De Sacra Venefica* circa 1947. "Uhm, no. Just no."

"What is it, Marigold?" Carver looked over my shoulder at the open tome on my kitchen counter.

My brother Rowan and nephew Michael sat at my weathered farmhouse table. It was surrounded by an assortment of mismatched chairs that I'd bought at garage sales and auctions. Today, they were working on perfecting their protection circles and sacred altars.

Not to brag, but I'd mastered those tasks in the first couple of weeks of lessons, so Carver let me move on to more complicated spells and potions. The current one was a guidance spell for a deity. Specifically, Hecate, the triple goddess. She was the goddess Carver worshipped, and according to him, she hadn't steered him wrong yet.

Only, I'd decided to change one or two of the elements for a different kind of guidance. I pointed to the passage in the book that had given me pause.

"Oh." Carver chuckled as he rubbed the bridge of his aquiline nose with the back of his index finger. "I don't think you have to get naked for the spell to work."

"Thank the universe," Rowan muttered.

Michael grunted his agreement as he drew a sigil outside his small protection circle. He tucked a sandy blond curl behind his ear. Now that the kid had graduated high school and was no longer playing sports, he was growing his hair. Frankly, he looked adorable.

I snorted a laugh. "Well, if there's a spell that requires me to strip, there better be a damn good reason and somebody better be holding a wad of bills to pay for the show." I winked at Carver, who laughed.

Michael had decided to ignore me as he finished his second sigil.

Rowan, a natural redhead with buttermilk skin and freckles, flushed a deep shade of crimson.

"You're going to give your brother a heart attack," Carver said.

"I guess it's a good thing he's a doctor then." I stuck my tongue out at Rowan. "Physician, heal thy self."

Rowan quit his private practice five months earlier to work as an emergency department doctor at Southill Memorial Hospital. He'd started working three ten-hour shifts a week and was on call day and night on those days. The new job allowed him more time to spend learning eclectic magic.

Carver had been staying at Rowan's house for the past few months, and I suspected more than rent was going on between them. My brother had always been private about his personal life, but I got the impression that he was more interested in the teacher than the lessons. I hadn't pried because I believed people were allowed to tell their truth in their own time. It was Rowan's life and his timeline. I only wanted his complete and utter happiness. Maybe Carver was the key.

My brother gave me a bland look, then cracked a smile. "There's no cure for pain in the ass sisters."

"Hah," I countered. "Too bad for you since you have three of them." We had an older sister, Dahlia, and two younger sisters, Iris and Rose. Rose, who had recently given birth to her third child, was taking what she liked to call a "maternity leave from magic."

My phone dinged, and more eager than I wanted to admit, I checked my messages. "Oh no." I frowned. "It's Justina."

"Bio sis?" Rowan asked.

I nodded. I'd never thought I would be interested in finding my biological family. After all, my mom had been the most wonderful mother I could've asked for, and I loved my fabulous dad with every fiber of my being. But last year, I'd been diagnosed with hereditary high blood pressure, so I'd taken a DNA test to see if there were any other medical conditions in my genetics that I needed to watch out for. I was only a few years from fifty. If there was one thing I knew for sure, it was that my health wasn't going to improve with age. Justina had also done a DNA test. We were a twenty-eight percent match.

"She's coming to Arkansas in a couple of weeks and wants to stop by for a visit."

"That's good, right?" Rowan asked. "You could introduce her to everyone."

I'd met Justina once. We shared the shapes of our noses and eyes, but she was shorter. Much shorter now that I'd gained five inches in height. I gestured up and down my body. "How am I supposed to explain my abnormal tallness?"

Michael tilted his head. "I grew four inches since graduation."

"You're a teenager who hasn't fully formed yet." I sighed. "I don't think that excuse will work for me."

"Are you planning on never seeing her again?" Carver asked.

"No," I told him. I liked Justina. We had the same father but different mothers. Our bio-dad had died five years ago, so I still had no idea about my birth mother. I was okay with not knowing. "I'd love to see her."

Carver's eyes brightened. "Then tell her yes."

"That easy, huh?"

"Besides," Rowan added. "Just tell her what you've told everyone around here."

My brow pinched. "That I have a rare, hereditary disorder that caused a midlife growth spurt?"

My brother grinned, then shrugged. "It's not a lie."

"I guess I could tell her it's hereditary on my maternal side." Which wasn't exactly a lie, either. Thanks to a near-death experience and a terrifying goddess, Macha, I was now a forest giant-human hybrid. The transformation had some unforeseen benefits for me when it occurred, like aging slower and the ability to talk to animals. But it also had its downside. I'd had to buy all new clothes...okay, maybe that went in the benefit column. But having people make tall jokes all the time wasn't fun.

I took my phone, battery down to thirty-two percent, into the living room and put it on the charger. As I walked back into the kitchen, I said, "I'll call her later. Let's just focus on the lesson." At the stove, I glanced at

Carver to see how closely he was watching me. When his gaze shifted to the table where the guys were spelling, I carefully threw a pinch of allspice into my spell pot.

Almost instantly, the bubbling green goo turned inky black. "Uhm…Should I be worried about this?" I probably should have asked before modifying the potion with a fire spice.

Carver craned his head over and nodded. "This doesn't look right. Did you add the mugwort?"

I grimaced, then bobbled my head in a slight but noncommittal shake-nod. "Not really." I grabbed a bamboo spoon from a utensil holder and stirred the potion. A caustic explosion, followed by a rain of noxious slime, made me yelp as I threw the spoon across the room.

"Disgusting," Michael got to his feet, waving his hand in front of his face. "I'm taking my lesson outside."

Rowan gagged as he followed suit. "Sorry, sis. I'm out, too."

"Save yourselves." I gagged as I wiped rotten egg-scented black slime from my face, then looked to Carver for help. "Why does it have to stink so bad?"

He narrowed his gaze on me. "Because you can't stir a fire spell with a wooden spoon."

"A fire spell?" I asked innocently.

"I can smell the allspice, Marigold." He groaned and plugged his nose. "You have to use the glass stirring rod with fire spells." Carver used a damp washcloth to wipe his face. "Never wood."

"I got distracted," I said in my defense, which, in

hindsight, was no defense at all. It wasn't just the text from my half-sister, though. I'd been having a lot of disruptive dreams of late that I couldn't get out of my head.

"I don't mind experimenting if you give me a heads up, but you have to use glass for fire potions," he instructed, "or things get..."

"Stinky," I supplied.

He shook his head. "At best." He handed me a glass stirring rod from the counter. "Look, if you're too distracted today, we can pick up the lesson tomorrow. It's not a big deal."

"I'm not distracted," I denied. "My attention is completely focused." Except for the reason I was working on a modified guidance spell in the first place—a certain ifrit whom I hadn't heard from in a long time. Of course, that hadn't stopped me from dreaming about him, and the dreams had become more frequent and intense in the past two months.

Carver's brow dipped as he took a towel from near my sink and wiped some of the potion slime from his shirt. "Is this about Zev?"

I averted my eyes. "Quit reading my mind."

"That's not in my skill set," he said. "However, I've noticed that in the last few lessons, you've been moving into more difficult spells, specifically about heat and fire resistance. It doesn't take a clairvoyant to put two and two together."

"I'm not doing the spells for Zev," I lied. One week

after he'd re-embraced his ifrit power, he'd sent me a text that said, *Remember, a part of me is always with you.* At first, I thought it was super sweet, but when I didn't hear from him again, that message became a scab that I couldn't stop picking. I resisted the urge to pull it up on my phone and read it for the gazillionth time. "He's out there living his best life, and I'm trying to do the same."

Carver looked at me sympathetically. "I'm sorry, Mare. I'm sorry you both had to sacrifice your relationship, but you know it was necessary. Zev did it to save your family."

I let out a noisy sigh. "I know." Knowing didn't make it hurt less. What Zev had done, embracing his fire to save my family, had bordered on heroic. He'd ensured that Bogmall, my sister's extremely powerful nemesis, would never escape her prison and wreak havoc on the people I loved ever again. But that heroism had made our love impossible. "I just wish he'd give me a sign that he's okay. We might not be able to be together, but it doesn't mean I don't want him in my life. Besides, he promised he'd come back."

"Marigold," Carver said, shaking me from my shame spiral. "Seven months isn't long for a creature that has lived for hundreds of years. He will come back."

"By your logic, I could be eighty...or dead by the time he returns." I chewed my thumbnail and tasted the allspice's bitterness. I tucked my hand into my left apron pocket where I'd put Zev's token and rubbed it like a worry stone. "But can you try to suspend logic for a moment? I understand all the reasons why he became an ifrit again and how it was an act of selflessness at great personal sacrifice."

"For both of you."

"But he promised me he'd be back, and not in forty years. I don't understand why he hasn't. He's a freaking djinn. He can apparate from one continent to the next. If he wanted to see me, he would make it happen." I could shake the memory of the Iron Grove, of the snotgurgle battle, almost dying, and Zev's declaration that he would grant me my every heart's desire. "There's something wrong. I can feel it. I keep seeing…" I shook my head. "My gut is worried."

"What does Iris say about your gut?"

Iris and Keir had gone on vacation to Ireland a few days earlier. I'd called her twice, but she hadn't answered. She'd sent a text last night to explain that she had crap reception and was still suffering jet lag, but it bothered me that I couldn't easily get ahold of her. Before she'd left for her vacation, I'd asked if she'd heard from Zev. She given me the same song and dance I'd been hearing for months. "Iris says that Zev texts her at least once a month to tell her that he's fine, and he'll return when he's ready."

"There you have it," Carver said as if that was all I needed to know.

"I don't buy it," I told him, fanning the air to dissipate the stench. "It's not like Zev to up and disappear." Though, could I claim to be an expert on the frustrating ifrit? I'd only known him for a short time. Even so, when I had been with him, it felt as if we'd known each other forever. "I'm so...angry and hurt and confused." More confused than anything else.

"I wish there were something I could do to make the pain easier, but other than a forget-me spell, which will make you forget him, there isn't anything that will help but time. And time marches to its own drummer." Carver made a face as some of the tarry green slime on the counter began to hiss. "We should get this goop cleaned up before it starts eating into your range."

I plucked the damp cloth from a hanging rack near the sink. "You have to admit, it's weird that he hasn't answered any of my texts. Not once. I haven't even seen the bouncing dots on the texts that will let you know when someone is at least considering messaging back." I wiped at the sticky mess. "I thought... No, I know that I meant more to him than that."

Carver grabbed another washcloth from my linen drawer. "You're both grieving a huge loss. But Zev's very old, and a broken heart takes longer to mend for him."

"But over seven months?" I shoved my hand into my apron pocket again and palmed the stone. "Come on. That's a long time for anyone, mortal or immortal."

Carver frowned. "I wish I knew what to say to make this better for you."

"I miss him. All the way to my core." I stopped scrubbing, and my eyes widened as I took in the fruit of my efforts. "Am I hallucinating, or is the black gunk starting to bubble and turn red?"

"You are definitely not hallucinating." Carver's normally laid-back tone was pinched. "We should run."

I gave him a sharp look. "What did you say?"

"Run!" He grabbed my arm and yanked me toward the back door.

When we made it outside, the explosion behind us flung me head-first into my Dwarf Burning Bush. Yes, I saw the irony.

I was dazed for a few seconds. I tried to focus. "Carver?" He didn't answer, and I worried the blast might've hurt him or worse. I groaned as the numbness of shock wore off, and pain scorched my left palm. I lifted my hand and saw several red, angry, and pointy triangles etched into my skin. I'd seen the symbol before. "Zev..." I muttered.

"I found her!" Michael yelled. "She's here!"

I reached up, grasping at the air as Rowan knelt beside me.

"Take it easy, grabby," he said. "Tell me where it hurts. Does anything feel broken?"

Only my heart, I thought, but saying it out loud wouldn't be helpful. "I'm okay." I moved my arms and legs to show him that I could. "Help me up."

Carver looked me over. "You've got a bruise on your forehead. Let's get you in the house where we can look you over properly."

I sagged against my brother when he hoisted me up. I was glad he was there to help keep me upright. I was also glad I still had a house.

All that work and research, and all I'd managed to make was a bomb. And for what? A pie-in-the-sky dream of finding a guy who wasn't acting like someone who wanted to be found. I felt pathetic. "I'm too old to be this stuck," I told Rowan as I shuffled toward the open door. "Why am I still pining for a guy I can't be with? Why can't I move on?"

"You have an unbridled zest for life, sis. You love hard and crash harder." He gave me a one-armed squeeze. "It's one of the many amazing things I've always admired about you."

"I'm not anyone to admire, Ro." I closed my eyes, longing for better times.

Rowan looped his arm under my back and stabilized me as we went inside. The door to the kitchen was still attached, but the cabinets above my antique stove were scorched, and the range had a black crater where the top had once been.

"I'll get the gas turned off," Rowan said as he reached behind the range for the shut-off valve.

"I already did," Carver told him. To me he said, "The good news is that the rest of the kitchen seems to be in good shape. Nothing that a good scrubbing with clean towels won't fix."

"Ha. Good plan." My hand throbbed with a persistent ache that wouldn't let me forget the pain. I glanced down at my palm. A large blister, about the size of a silver dollar, had formed, obscuring the pattern that had been there before. Had I imagined it?

"We need to get that under cold water, then clean it and wrap it," Rowan said. It's definitely second-degree."

"Good thing I have a private concierge doctor on duty."

"Dr. Everlee, at your service." He chuckled. "I won't even charge you an emergency fee."

Michael turned the cold water on for me, but I got lightheaded and wobbly when I tried to walk to the sink.

"Whoa," Rowan cautioned. "Take it easy." He assisted me to the running tap. "You got thrown a fair way. You might have a concussion. Maybe Carver has something for that, too." He glanced at the tall eclectic witch, who was fervently wiping black gunk from my cabinet doors.

I smiled as I put my hand under the running tap and quietly said, "Maybe it's time you tried out that unbridled zest for life you're so enamored by."

His flushed cheeks made me grin.

"Hey," I told Carver. "I'll clean up later. You don't have to—"

The eclectic witch turned sharply to look at me. "I've uncovered something strange under the scorch marks." He gestured toward the blackened cabinets like Vanna White displaying a vowel. On the doors above the stove, distinct lines had been burned into the surface.

"The triangles." I turned the water off. "Zev's triangles." I rubbed my palm. "The same pattern was burned into my hand."

"There's no pattern on your palm. Just a major blister," Rowan said.

"But it was there," I insisted. I reached into my pocket to show them the stone, but it wasn't there. Crap. Had it fallen out somewhere outside when I'd been tossed during the explosion? "I had a rock." I indicated my apron pocket. "It was Zev's. It had the same symbols on it."

"Okay, the symbols make a little more sense now," Carver said slowly. "The writing is cuneiform. It means soul stone of fire, or something to that effect. It's not a perfect translation."

"You know cuneiform?" Rowan asked him. "Isn't it a dead language?"

"I know a lot of things." Carver arched his brow as he held Rowan's gaze for a moment, then turned to me. "What did you do to the potion? This shouldn't have been a side effect of the spell you were brewing."

"I was trying to find Zev. To get a message to him. Or get one from him. Nonmagical means weren't working, so I was trying something new. I had no idea the spell would go full nuclear in my kitchen." If I had, I would have brewed it outside over a campfire.

Carver gave a slight head shake. "There's another symbol over here." He indicated some extra lines and waves to the side of the triangles.

My heartbeat had kicked into fourth gear. "What does it say?"

Carver's hand dropped to his side, and he put his

hand on my shoulder. "Caught," he said. Again, not a perfect translation."

"I knew it," I said with full vindication. "It's a message from Zev." I looked at Carver. "He's in trouble," I told him. "And he needs my help."

Come hell or high water, he was going to get it.

Chapter Three

I COULDN'T BELIEVE THIS WAS HAPPENING. THE spell had worked. It had actually freaking worked. I flicked my hand in the direction of the symbols. "Don't you get it? He's in trouble."

"That's a bit of a reach," Rowan said skeptically. "We know he's been in contact with Iris. How much trouble can he be in?"

"Do we?" I walked outside, looking around my backyard for Zev's token. I knew in my heart this was a sign from him, and I had to figure out a way to prove it.

"What are you doing?" Carver asked.

"Aunt Marigold?" Michael's tone was hesitant. "Are you okay?"

"No, I'm not." A noise of frustration escaped me. "I've lost the stone."

Rowan was stooped over, examining the grass. "What stone? One of your crystals?"

"A shiny black rock with red veins. It's the size of a quarter and looks like a skipping stone." I fought back a sob. "It was a gift from Zev."

Carver's brow knitted as his eyes narrowed to slits. "Does this stone have symbols on the surface?"

I held out my hand. "Did you find it?"

He shook his head. "No, but it sounds like a *sebtusiptu*."

My eyes widened and my stomach turned a somersault. "That's what Zev called it. He said it meant token."

"Of what?" Michael asked.

"His esteem," I answered.

Carver tugged at his ear. "Not exactly."

"I'm not seeing anything like that," Rowan declared from several feet away. "I'll check the bushes."

"We need to find it," Carver said. "If it's really Zev's *sebtusiptu*, we have to find it. Zev's freedom could depend on it."

"I don't understand."

"A *sebtusiptu* is a token of debt," Carver explained. "The djinn who makes it imbues the stone with a piece of their soul."

"His soul." My knees turned rubbery, and I reached out and grasped Carver's arm to steady myself. "Right before he gave it to me, he had said he owed Freya a debt and that it had been paid." I clenched my fist and winced as the painful burn screamed against my palm. I shook my hand. "He said to keep it, and a part of him would always be with me."

"If it's his token, then he was telling the truth. A piece of him is in that stone."

I shook my head, feeling like I might puke. "I didn't know he was being literal." I wouldn't have carried it around in my pocket like a trinket if I had. "If he'd told me, I would've taken more care."

Carver's gaze met mine. "If I know you, and I think I do, you have known where that stone is every minute of the day since Zev left Southill."

"Not over here," Rowan said from the fire bush.

"We should do a grid search," Michael suggested.

"Have you been watching true crime shows?" Rowan asked.

"Archeologists use grids to unearth ancient treasures," Michael replied. After a moment's hesitation, he added with some chagrin, "But yes, I've been watching true crime shows."

I chuckled and then gave my nephew a grateful look. "The blast threw me about ten feet. We should start with the bush and work our way out."

"That's not exactly how a grid works," Michael muttered. "But sure."

I smacked his shoulder with my good hand. "Less whining, more looking."

He haphazardly saluted me with two fingers. "Okay, boss."

I nudged him with my hip. "That's Aunt Boss to you."

The earth beneath my feet stirred, a subtle movement

unnoticed by the guys. A second later, the ground parted, revealing a tiny nose resembling a delicate flower, sniffing the air with curiosity. "Mareee-gool," the creature chirped. "Hear boom."

"Hi, Tupo," I greeted the little mole with a nod. "Big boom."

It was strange to think that just a year ago, I'd attempted to deter these burrowing creatures with wind spinners and whirligigs planted all over my yard. Who knew forest giants were fluent in critter-speak? Since then, I had abandoned the futile attempts to get rid of Tupo and embraced coexistence with him. Knowing the name of my tiny neighbor had made evicting him unsavory. Even so, I'd established ground rules, particularly regarding tunneling near my kitchen. Most of the time, I only had Tupo to contend with, but February began mating season for the little fellow. Moles didn't mate for life, but Tupo had found himself a temporary missus. She'd given birth to three newborn pups at the end of March.

Tupo wiggled his nose and hoisted himself up with his clawed hands. His dark brown fur contrasted sharply with his light beige hands and pink nose. "Boom scared babies," he complained.

"I'm sorry," I apologized sincerely. "It was an accident."

He cocked his head to the side. "Done now?" he inquired.

"All done," I reassured him with more confidence

than I felt. "Hey, could you and your family keep an eye out for a flat, round, shiny black stone with red veins?"

"Yes, for Mari-gool." With a wave of his hands, Tupo disappeared back into the earth, leaving me to wonder if my request would be remembered amidst the daily adventures of mole life.

"You're such a weirdo," Rowan said.

"I'm rubber, and you're glue, bro."

He laughed. "I'll never get used to you talking to animals. What did that one say?"

"Tupo said he could smell your butt from a mile away."

"Har har." Rowan rolled his eyes. "What did it really say?"

"He," I corrected. "Tupo wanted to know about the explosion. He said it scared his kids. He'd wanted to make sure I was done blowing crap up."

"Oh." His expression pinched. "It's still weird."

"You're weird."

"You're both weird," Michael said. "Argue less, search more."

"Found something." Carver plucked an object from the ground and brushed the dust off. "Wait, no. It's the right size and shape, according to your description, but no red veins or symbols."

I strode over to him with my hand out. "Let me see."

He pressed it into my palm, and I shivered at the familiar feel and weight. He was right, there were no veins, no symbols. But, as I rubbed my thumb across the surface, I knew without a doubt that this was Zev's token. My pulse quickened. The spell must've changed the token somehow. If a piece of Zev's soul was in there, had I killed it? Would that harm Zev in some way? "I... I think I broke it."

"Is it the right one?" Rowan asked, peering around me for a better view. "It looks like a worry stone."

I'd carried the token with me every day since Zev gave it to me. I could identify it with my eyes closed. "It's the right one. But it's wrong. Changed." I flipped it over. "It used to have three red lines that kind of looked like the number four, and..." I turned it over again. "There were pointy triangles on this side, like the ones on the cabinet doors. Veining too, but thinner, more weblike."

The adrenaline of losing Zev's stone had started to wane, and my hand began to throb. I lifted my left hand to look at the burn. The blister stuck out a half-inch from my palm and was the size of a silver dollar.

"It looks like it's filling up with blood," Carver said. "We better treat it before it gets worse."

I tucked the stone back into my pocket. "We need to find out what's going on with Zev."

"We will," Rowan assured me. "But if you don't get that hand treated, I'll have to amputate. You don't want me breaking out the bone saw."

"Fine." I knew he was teasing, but the fiery pain was getting distracting. "I'm happy to let you two play Doctors."

An interesting look flashed between them—a look I

planned to interrogate them about later. For now, I had enough of my own personal intrigue to keep me busy.

As we walked back into the kitchen, I grimaced at the mess. I'd blown up my stove and ruined Zev's rock. What was I going to screw up next?

Rowan helped me to the sink. "Run your hand under that cold water for another minute or two."

"Do you have aloe vera, lavender, chamomile, and witch hazel?" Carver asked. "I didn't bring my herb kit."

"I could go get it for you," Rowan offered. "It wouldn't take long to run home."

"You wouldn't mind?" the eclectic witch asked. Their shyness with each other made me think that if anything was going on it was relatively new. A flash of giddiness and the cold running water briefly distracted me from the pain.

"No need." I gestured with my non-injured hand. "I have all those ingredients. Lavender is hanging there." I pointed to the drying rack in the window. Aloe vera is in the front yard rock garden by my driveway." I reached up and opened the cabinet above my sink and took a box down. "Et voilà. Chamomile tea. Oh, and the witch hazel is in the bathroom medicine cabinet."

Carver arched a brow at me.

"I use it for my pores," I explained.

"Ah, right," he said. "Well, then, I think we have all the ingredients. Rowan and Michael, can you get the aloe and witch hazel? I'll get the two ingredients here in the kitchen."

"You got it." Rowan gestured to Michael. "You get the aloe."

"Works for me," the teenager quipped. Gosh, Michael had grown up so much in the last year. Learning your mother was a tru-craft witch and that her life was in constant danger had a way of putting life into perspective. I know Iris was disappointed when Michael decided to take a gap year from college to learn more about his heritage and explore magic, but I couldn't have been prouder of him.

Carver grabbed his tool bag and set it on the table. "Mortar and pestle?"

"Does material matter?"

Carver's mouth widened in a grin. "You're starting to think like a witch."

I returned the smile. "High praise indeed." I pointed across the kitchen to the far wall. "There's a clean black granite mortar and pestle on the shelf to the left of my oven mitts."

"Excellent. Black granite is perfect for a healing spell." He gathered the tea, lavender, mortar, and pestle and set them near his bag. While he prepared to make his magical salve, he offhandedly asked, "What were you trying to achieve with the spell?"

I was glad he hadn't accused me of being reckless, but it didn't stop me from feeling like a fool. "I'm sorry, Carver. I know it was stupid to change the spell."

He looked at me quizzically. "I'm not angry with

you." He pulled a chair out for me. "Come over here and sit."

I reluctantly turned the water off because my hand started to sting again. I waved it at my side to let the air cool the surface as I strolled over and took the seat.

Carver sat down in the chair next to mine and leaned toward me. "You accomplished powerful magic, Marigold. You have the gift. Tell me about your thought process. I want to know exactly what you changed and hoped to achieve with the spell."

How could I explain something about which I wasn't completely certain? "I've had this gut feeling for months that something was off with Zev. I've been researching the books you gave me and some spell books I found online. The guidance spell, from my understanding, is designed to send a message to someone who can't be reached by normal means."

"But just because he hasn't called you doesn't mean Zev's been unreachable. Iris said he's been communicating with her."

"Yeah," I said skeptically, "but has he? The occasional brief text message isn't really communication." I shook my head. "The last thing he said 'Remember, a part of me is always with you' , then nothing. He's not the kind of guy who would do that. Not to me."

Carver's brows dipped. "Regardless of what Zev would or wouldn't do, tell me more about the spell." He used a small pair of scissors to snip the dried lavender flowers into the mortar bowl. Afterward, he cut open a tea bag and dumped the chamomile inside. He used the pestle to grind the dried herbs as he waited patiently for me to answer.

"You're a good man," I said, surprising both of us.

He gave me a lopsided smile. "Uh, thanks."

"I mean it. You should be outraged right now. You're trying to teach me magic, and I'm playing Russian Roulette with a difficult potion."

He shook his head. "Is that how you deal with your students when they use their brains, imagination, and innovation to increase the scope of their knowledge?"

I chuckled. "No one blows up a stove because someone has drawn a correlative comparison between Madame Curie and Marge Simpson's impact on modern feminism." I waved off the notion. I'd taught Women's Studies at Darling University for fourteen years and had never seen that correlation, but it made my point. "I'm not sure it's a fair comparison."

"Okay," he conceded. "So, I take it you were trying to get a message to Zev. What ingredients did you use to change the spell, and why did you think they would work?"

I glanced out the window and saw Michael coming up the walk. "I saw that the guidance spell had a lot of similar ingredients to a message or communication potion —bay leaf, dandelion, and such. So, I, uh, I exchanged allspice for the yarrow and added a pinch of dried hibiscus."

"Hibiscus?" He narrowed his gaze at me. "That's an herb for love spells."

I shrugged. "I was trying to reach someone specific."

"That you were." Carver looked up past me, and the tension around his eyes eased. "Ah, Rowan. Great." He held out his hand and took the offered bottle from my brother.

Michael came in with three long aloe stalks. "I hope this is enough."

"Perfect," Carver told him. "Get a knife, slice the leaves in half, then scrape the insides onto a plate and bring it here." He unscrewed the cap on the witch hazel and poured a small amount into the bowl with the pulverized flowers.

Michael brought the plate with the aloe gel he'd procured and set it on the table. Carver took a small wooden spatula with a twisty carved handle from his tool kit and scooped the clear slime into the mixture.

"This seems less magical and more holistic," I said skeptically.

My mentor raised a brow at me. "Now for the magic." He stirred counterclockwise five times. "Give me your hand."

I held it out. He dipped two fingers in the bowl.

I winced and tugged my hand away when it looked like he was going to rub the goo on my blister. "Maybe Rowan could shoot me up with lidocaine first."

Carver shook his head. "Trust me?"

I glanced at Rowan. He raised a brow. "I don't carry

lidocaine or syringes on me, so maybe you should just trust him."

"Aren't you supposed to be all science is boss when it comes to medical care?" My hand pulsated with pain.

Rowan laughed. "Magic is just science that hasn't been discovered yet."

Carver took my hand and gently circled the blister with the salve he'd made. He drew a triskaideka in the center and chanted, "Hecate, wise and calm, grace to mend the blistered palm. Goddess of magic, good health to receive, using herbs to soothe this burn, let pain leave."

I gasped as the intense burning sensation began to subside, but the edges of the blister still throbbed with discomfort. I heard Michael behind me say, "Wow. I'd like to see the science that explains that."

Carver smiled as he finished his incantation: "Mother of witchcraft, grace your daughter, my friend. Take her hand in yours and help her mend."

My eyes shot wide as I watched the blister get smaller and smaller until it was gone, but what it left behind surprised everyone.

Black triangles with red veining lines decorated the healed skin.

"The symbols." Carver brushed his thumb over my palm. "It's like they're tattooed into your skin."

"That's the same thing on the wall," Rowan added.

"It sure is." I stared at the pointy triangles that had once been on the stone in my pocket. I shifted my gaze to Carver. "What does it mean?"

"I'm not sure." He stood up while retrieving his phone from his bag. "But I'll make a few calls and see what I can find out."

I wasn't going to idly wait for Carver's contacts to come through. If Zev was in trouble, I needed answers and fast. Iris had been evasive about Zev's texts, and I'd let it go because I knew she'd been trying to protect my heart. I had to know the last time the ifrit had messaged her and what he said. More importantly, I had to know if he'd clued her into his whereabouts.

I got up and marched into the living room, where my phone was plugged into the charger then tapped on Iris's number.

"Hah, you missed me, bitch," Iris's voice sang out. "If you're not spam, political, or a robocall, leave a brief message after the beep, and I'll get back to you."

This was the third call in two days that had gone to voicemail. After the tone, I quietly said, "Are you screening my messages? Stuff is going down here of the magical variety, and I'm pretty sure Zev's in the shit. Call me ASAP or, so help me, I will fly to Ireland for a good old-fashioned sister smackdown." I paused before I disconnected and added, "I love you. I'm scared. Call me."

Chapter Four

Carver wrapped up his call. Excitement sparked in his eyes as he turned to face us. "I talked to Ryker, a djinnologist I know. She's agreed to help investigate," he announced, his voice tinged with anticipation.

"Did you say gemologist?" Michael arched his brows.

"A djinnologist," Carver corrected. "Ryker is an expert on djinns and genies. She's my go-to person when it comes to all things djinn-related."

"Ah. Okay. That makes way more sense," my nephew said. "Got it."

Djinnology was something I was deeply interested in learning more about. I had no idea it was a field someone could study. I leaned forward and asked, "How did Ryker become an expert on djinns?"

Carver leaned against my kitchen counter. He brushed a hand through his hair before explaining, "The same way you become an expert on anything—years of dedicated learning and a knack for unraveling mysteries."

Recalling Zev's stories about the enigmatic nature of djinns, I expressed my skepticism. "Djinns aren't known for sharing their secrets freely."

Carver nodded, a knowing glint in his eyes. "Ryker's not exactly your average human."

"In what way?" I pressed, intrigued by the cryptic hint.

"She's a bit like you and me. Half human and half supernatural." He gave me a slight smile. "Ryker's mother was human, and her father was marid, a powerful race of djinn who have a strong connection to nature and magic," Carver explained. "They used to be sought out by kings and queens as advisors."

Unlike Carver who was half sylph, I hadn't been born a half-giantess. That had been Macha's doing. She'd taken the less than one percent of my DNA that had been forest giant and multiplied the heck out of it. "Did Ryker know about her lineage from the beginning?" I asked, fascinated by the unfolding story.

Carver shook his head, his expression solemn. "Ryker's mother passed away when she was seventeen. If her mom knew the truth, she never shared it with her," he explained. "The revelation only came when Ryker turned forty and still looked twenty. Her father showed up and told her she would have to change her name and move every fifteen to twenty years if she didn't want to draw attention to the fact that she wasn't growing old. That was twenty-eight years ago."

"Sixty-eight but looking twenty?" Rowan shook his head incredulously. "I need a djinn-daddy." He grimaced and flushed as he glanced at Carver. "I didn't mean that the way it sounded."

I chuckled at Rowan's slip, enjoying the banter.

Rowan shot me a dirty look then redirected the conversation. "So, tell us more about Ryker."

Michael gave his uncle a pat on the back. "Nice segue."

My brother shot our nephew a look. "Pretty sure I didn't ask for an opinion.

Michael grinned and gave him a thumbs up.

The marid might be a wise race, but this one wasn't going to win any father-of-the-year awards. That was another reason to be grateful I'd never met my biological parents. "That has to be a hard way to live for Ryker."

Carver nodded his agreement. "Ryker ignored her father. She'd do a lot of work remotely. It's not hard to hide your near-immortality if you don't get close to anyone."

"How sad," Michael said, his voice tinged with sympathy.

"Living that long can be lonely," Carver said soberly. He gave me a sly look. "I'm over a hundred years old."

My brother choked and coughed. "Inhaled spit wrong," he rasped, his face contorted in a mixture of surprise and disbelief.

Carver chuckled. "Kidding. I'm only thirty-nine." He winked at me. "For the past sixty-one birthdays."

Rowan's eyes bugged, but this time he could see Carver was joking. He rolled his eyes.

My poor brother. He was completely enamored of the eclectic witch. I hoped the feeling was mutual. "What can marids do?" I asked. "Magic-wise, I mean."

Carver walked over, sat at the table, and spread his hands. "That's the race of djinn that all the genies in lamp lore are based on. They will grant three wishes to anyone clever enough to trap them. They can also detect magic and the paranormal in the world."

"Did your friend inherit any of the marid's abilities? Can Ryker grant wishes?" Zev had told me that nothing is free when it comes to wishes.

"Ryker has a long life expectancy, of course, and she can detect magic and magical creatures, but she can't apparate from one place to the other. Like most people, she has to walk, drive, or fly if she wants to go somewhere."

I gave my phone a slight shake to wake up the screen. It was nearly noon. "When is she coming?"

Carver spread his hands. "She's in Kentucky tracking a Kelly goblin tormenting a family living near Licking River."

"None of that sounds like a real thing," Michael told him. "Kelly goblin on Licking River. Who is coming up with these names?"

"And it doesn't answer the question about when she's

coming," I pointed out. "If Zev's in trouble, we have to act now."

"If you have any suggestions as to where we could start, I'm happy to hear you out." Carver tipped his head to me.

I flipped him the bird then shrugged. "I could try the spell again."

My suggestion was met with a chorus of "no!" from the guys.

"Fine. Gah. You blow up one stove, and nobody lets you live it down." I knew they were right. Exploding more stuff in the house wasn't the solution, but my heart ached, not knowing what was happening to Zev. The cryptic symbol for "caught" was the only clue I had to go on, and it wasn't enough. My frustration mounted. There was nothing worse than feeling utterly powerless. If only there was a spell to conjure real answers, but life and magic weren't that simple. Still, I clung to hope, desperate to find a way to free him from whatever trouble he was in. "So, how long until Ryker gets here?"

Carver nodded. "She said she was close to wrapping up the job and would be here by morning."

Rowan looked at the demolished stove and then at me. "You could stay the night at my place if you want."

"Or mine," Michael added.

"Thank you. Both of you. I think I'm going to stay home."

Now it was Carver's turn to look skeptical. Or maybe it was suspicion. "Marigold, you shouldn't be alone."

"I'm not going to try the spell again," I said. "Promise." I crossed my fingers under the table to give myself some wiggle room.

"I can stay," Michael told Carver. "I'll sleep on the pullout sofa."

In a dramatic pose, I touched my forehead with the back of my hand. "Et tu, Michael?"

"We can spend the evening going down a Google rabbit hole," he offered.

"Enticing," I admitted. A few years ago, I'd been diagnosed with ADHD, and hyper-focusing on internet searches for random stuff that popped into my head was a great way to raise my dopamine levels and get me out of my funk. "You'd help me do research?"

"Of course, Auntie." His smile was earnest. "I'd do anything for you."

"Because I'm your favorite aunt?"

"Sure," he replied with a smirk.

"Don't worry. I won't tell Rose." Dahlia wouldn't care, but Rose was hormonal at the moment.

"So, it's settled then." Carver got up from his seat. "Before Rowan and I go, we'll help you clean up the mess." He looked at the stove and the black goo and smoke damage. "Well, as much as we can."

"Can I leave while you do it?" Cleaning was my least favorite chore.

"Not happening," my brother said. He grabbed a washcloth from the drawer near my sink and threw it at me. "Let's go, girl."

Michael chimed in with a naughty smirk. "She who smelt is dealt it. Therefore, she has to deal with it."

I rolled my eyes. "I didn't fart."

"Sure smells like you did," he pointed out... correctly.

Despite feeling somewhat out of control, I laughed. Grabbing a rag, I joined the cleaning party. My nephews logic might stink, but it was accurate.

*****

The internet had surprisingly little information on djinns. I had known that from previous searches, but I'd hoped Michael would have some Google ninja skills to find the secret paranormal dark web. Long story short, he didn't. However, time passed so fast. Another benefit of ADHD was time blindness. If I was doing something interesting, five hours could feel like five minutes. At two o'clock in the morning, we called it a night.

I got undressed and put Zev's blank stone on my bedside table. I rubbed my palm and still couldn't believe that his symbol had imprinted onto my skin. There weren't any raised lines, just solid black lines depicting several triangles arranged in an order that I'd memorized since I'd been given the smooth, round rock. The red lines weren't like blood veins; the red was too bright for that.

"What does it all mean?" I uttered. I'd been so upset when I'd found the token blank, and I'll admit, I was strangely relieved when Carver's healing spell revealed and confirmed the cuneiform writing had transferred to my palm. I felt as if I still had something of Zev's with me. The rock was cold, but my hand was warm. I pressed the symbol over my heart. "Zev, where are you?"

As I drifted to sleep, his face, lips, hands, and body were on my mind. I remembered the way he would whisper in my ear in a language that I couldn't understand, but, oh man, those words were filled with so much promise. We'd spent three heated nights together before he embraced his fire, and during those three nights, I'd experienced more love and passion than I had in my entire adult life.

"I would not do this, libbu ša, if it weren't necessary to keep you and your family safe. I need you to understand," Zev stroked the side of my cheek. His gaze melted my core. *"Please say you understand."*

"I do," I told him. *"Of course, I do."* He'd used his magic to make himself taller to match my new height. I slid my hands behind his neck and interlaced my fingers. I fought back the tears hot in my eyes. *"I think what you're doing to save Iris, and really, to save all of us is so brave."* I croaked as a sob jumped to my throat. *"I don't want this to be the end for us."*

"I don't want that either, my heart. You have become...important to me. I never want that to change."

"But it will change, won't it?" I couldn't meet his gaze. *"If you're fire, we can't be together."*

"We'll cross that road after we put Bogmall in a very deep, dark hole."

"Will you take her right away?"

He nodded, his brown eyes going almost black. "I will take her to my people, but I will return."

"Promise?"

"I will do everything in my power to come back to...Southill as soon as possible."

"And we'll still be friends?" I asked. "Even though we can't..." I made a low whistle sound.

His kissable lips tugged into a smile. "Yes, even if we can't..." He dipped his head, his mouth brushing over mine.

Electricity tingled through me and made a beeline for my groin. I moaned as I leaned into the kiss. Zev's tongue slid across the part in my lips, and I opened for him as the kiss deepened. Oh, god. This would be the last time I'd ever be kissed by this man. I wanted the moment to last forever. But I knew it wouldn't. It couldn't. Soon, Zev would say goodbye, and that would be the end.

"I am a part of you, libbu ša. You have my heart and my soul, and as long as you keep them safe—keep them with you—then I am never truly lost."

"I will keep you with me," I told him. "Always."

"I know you will." He caressed my neck before lifting my hand. He turned my palm up before tracing the triangle symbols with the tip of his finger. "It's time to wake up," he said, then added, "Find me, Marigold."

I narrowed my gaze, my brow furrowed. "Where are you?"

"Caught," Zev replied.

"Between a rock and a hard place?"

"Between a liar and a thief." His gaze went far off. "I can't see my location but find the hunter."

"Who's the hunter?" I was confused. We were saying goodbye. I'd had this dream over and over of our last conversation in Iris's backyard, but now the ending had changed. "What's happening?"

"I can't stay, my darling. If I do, he'll find you. I can't let him know that you're important to me. He'll use you to get what he wants from me."

The hunter? This wasn't how our goodbye had ended.

Zev's smile disappeared. "He's coming. Wake up, Marigold."

"Wake up, Marigold." Not Zev's voice. Rowan's. "Carver's friend will be here in about fifteen minutes. She's ten miles south of town."

I blinked and gave my brother a death stare.

"Wow. What were you dreaming about?"

I quickly got out of bed. "Don't talk to me. I don't want to forget." Dreams slipped away as time passed. Even seconds could kill one. I couldn't let that happen, especially since this dream could hold the clue to finding Zev. I knew in my heart that Zev had managed to get me another message.

I grabbed my dream journal from the nightstand and

removed the pen from inside it. I wrote down everything I could remember.

I looked at my brother, annoyed he'd dragged me out of the dream. What if Zev had more to tell me? "What's going on?"

"Good question," my brother muttered. He shook his head. "Carver's friend. She'll be here in fifteen minutes."

Chapter Five

After jotting down what I could recall of the dream, I gave the notes to Rowan to show Carver, then took a quick shower and threw on some clothes. Carver had brewed a pot of coffee, a lifesaver for my groggy brain. The eclectic witch, who barely glanced at me when I walked in, was at my kitchen table reading my dream notes. The smell of fried dough and sweet goodness hit me right away.

It turned out that Michael was the real hero of the morning. The young man had ventured out early to Southill Sweets and Treats. He'd returned bearing an array of donuts, among which he'd snagged a cinnamon twist just for me. I wasted no time sinking my teeth into its crispy exterior and pillowy interior, relishing every delightful bite.

"Thanks a bunch," I grinned at Michael between

mouthfuls. "You'll definitely get a shout-out in my will for this."

He clicked his tongue. "Just don't leave me the El Camino."

"That old beast is a classic." I defended my car. "It's got the utility of a truck and the comfort of a car."

"It clunks when you shift gears, and the engine smokes whenever you make a right turn." Michael's expression remained unimpressed. "Besides, that cruck is fugly."

I turned to my brother for backup, but he shook his head. "Can't argue with him on that one."

"Can't or won't?" I pouted. "A race car driver I once had a fling with gave me that El Camino."

"Demolition derbies aren't exactly racing," my brother pointed out. "And let's not forget the restraining order you had to take out on him because he wouldn't leave you alone. Don't act like it holds a lot of sentimental value."

"Hey, it was a fun couple of months before he got creepy." I took another healthy bite of the donut and made the *mmm* sound the confection deserved.

Carver chuckled. "You had a stalker."

"More than one," Rowan tattled.

Michael smirked. "I overheard mom say Aunt Marigold was a trouble magnet. She has a thing for dangerous dudes."

I would've protested, but the kid wasn't wrong. There was something thrilling about men who took risks.

I'd since learned that my choices of companions were probably a direct result of my ADHD. Hot, horny, violent, and sometimes obsessive men stirred up those dopamine levels like a sweet, sweet drug. Even so, I'd never fallen in love. Not with a single one of them. It made breakups very easy—for me, anyhow.

The last couple of years, with a little help from medication and a lot of help from therapy, I'd been celibate, minus the occasional hook-up with BOB. And no, not the cuddly cat who kept my sister company. BOB was my battery-operated boyfriend. Bonus, I'd never have to take a restraining order out on him. Was that why I liked Zev so much? Because he was dangerous? The thought was sobering.

From the outside, it could look that way. I knew Iris had worried for me and my safety when it came to the ifrit. She'd been wrong. Zev was the gentlest, kindest man I'd ever met. He detested violence, even if he was seriously good at fighting. The first time we met, I tried to attack Zev at Iris's house. I smiled at the memory. I'd lunged at him with my hair pins akimbo and tripped on the steps to Iris's front porch. The sly ifrit hadn't tried to stop me. He'd merely stepped out of the way and let me fall. On my face.

When he'd given me his hand to help me up from the ground, my whole body and brain had lit up with fireworks. I think I knew then and there that my celibacy streak wasn't going to last. Of course, at the time, I had no idea of the hurdles I'd have to jump in order to get into his pants.

"Are you sure he said to find the hunter?" Carver asked as he set the notes down.

"Yeah, that's what he said. But do you have any idea who or what he could be talking about?" I frowned, worry creeping into my voice. "Unless it's just my mind trying to rationalize all the weird shit." I flipped my hand over and traced the ifrit's symbol. "What if all this is just some manifestation of my desire to have Zev back?"

"It's possible," Carver said. "Even so, it won't cost us anything but some research time to find out if this hunter is someone of note in the supernatural world."

A knock sounded on my front door. "Oh, Ryker's here!" I scooted out of my chair and dusted cinnamon and sugar crumbs from my shirt. Anticipation and excitement got me moving. I had so many questions for Carver's djinn expert.

I practically flung the door open, my eyes wide. The person standing on my stoop was tall and thin, and for the first time in my life, I understood the term "willowy" as it pertained to someone's body type. Ryker had bright purple hair, shaved up on the sides but longer on top. She wore brown cargo pants, black combat boots, and a white Rockpalast Patti Smith sleeveless crewneck t-shirt. Ryker had clear, smooth, light brown skin, dark expressive eyes that were slightly wide, making them even more striking, a sharp, small nose, and high cheekbones. She might be sixty-eight years old, but she looked like a teenager.

"Hi," Ryker greeted with her hand extended. "You must be Marigold."

"You are stunning," I blurted.

She gave me a quick wink. "I bet you say that to all the djinns."

I grinned. "So far, I'm two for two." I gestured inside. "Come on in."

Carver embraced his friend. "It's been too long."

"You don't call. You don't write," Ryker teased as she held the hug.

Carver's face lit up with pleasure, and I could see my brother's expression protectively go blank. Uh oh. I recognized jealousy when I saw it.

The pair of old friends were speaking what sounded like quiet babble. I took it upon myself to interrupt the reunion. "So, how did you all meet?"

Ryker gave Carver a friendly pat and then let him go. "When Carver was seventeen, he worked at a coffee shop in Cedarburg, Wisconsin. I was at UMW." She tilted her head, and her bangs fell into her eyes. She brushed them back. "University of Milwaukee-Wisconsin. Cedarburg was a twenty-minute drive north, but I liked the quiet of the small town." She gave Carver a fond look.

"I've heard of UMW," I told her. "I work at Darling University, where I'm the head of women's studies. I mean, I was. I recently took some time off." I waved my hand. "But go on, please. I have a bad habit of interrupting."

"It's fine." Ryker's eyes were alight with amusement. "I noticed Carver right away."

"I'm sure you did," Rowan mumbled, then back-tracked in embarrassment. "I mean, he's extremely tall, so he's easy to spot."

Ryker laughed, "You're right. He does stand out in a crowd, but that's not why I noticed him. I have a gift for reading magical auras. I was in my late 40s at the time, and I was having a journey of self-discovery and in the height of my research of the paranormal and supernatural world. I have a knack for identifying magic, and with Carver, I could see his so clearly. He was half tru-craft half sylph."

"Ah." I looked at Carver. "That's how you knew Thomas was your father."

He inclined his head. "It was part of the unraveling, but not all of it."

"I would stop by the shop every weekend during his senior year to study, and he started up a conversation with me on one of his breaks." Her tone reflected her fondness for the eclectic witch. "This went on for several months until he asked me about my work. I can't explain it, but for the first time in a long time, I found myself trusting somebody who wasn't me. I told Carver everything."

"She helped me as much as I helped her," Carver added.

I could see my brother fighting to come back with another snarky comment. I wanted to applaud his self-control when he refrained from saying, "I bet you did," and simply nodded.

"I could see his magic in the same way that I see yours." Her head tilted side to side as she studied me up and down. "Giant. Mmm-hmm. Forest if the shade of green is any indication. But there's something else..."

"Witch," I provided. I might not be able to manipulate elements like my sister Iris, but she'd made me part of her coven, and in doing so, I'd become part of the supernatural world. "Carver said you could see magic, but I didn't realize you could identify the kind of magic. You're good. I'm part forest giant."

"While you do have a slight essence so witch, that's not what I'm seeing." She held up her fine boned, delicate hands in front of me. "May I?"

I tucked my chin. "Are you going to read the bumps on my head? Because I've had my skull felt up by a holistic shaman into phrenology."

Ryker's face registered mild surprise.

"I dated him...briefly."

"Not dangerous enough," Rowan commented.

I gave him a scathing glance. He smirked.

"Any-hoodles," I continued. "He said I was a pushy bitch."

Ryker shook her head and tried not to smile. "I can see why your relationship was brief."

"Dude had a death wish," Michael said.

"Hello," she said to Michael. "And who are you?"

Her look was nearly as curious as when she'd been staring at me.

"Michael Everlee," my nephew said. His expression matched Ryker's. I'll admit Ryker was alluringly attractive, but while she might look young, she was technically forty-eight years older than Michael.

I cleared my throat. "Uh, back over here. Go ahead and read my bumps."

Ryker barked a laugh. "I don't actually have to touch you. Your bumps are safe. I just want to test your aura."

"For what?" Carver asked.

"There's more to Marigold than giant and human. It's muddy, though. I need to feel the magic."

"Okay." I pinched my bottom lip between my teeth, reached into my pocket, and nervously worried Zev's stone. When the goddess had changed me, I'd been saturated in snotgurgle ooze. What if some of it made it into my new DNA? I held up my right hand and said, "If you find any troll in my aura, you can keep that shit to yourself."

"No worries. I detect no troll."

"That's a good start." My shoulders relaxed. "Give it to me straight, Doc. I can take it."

Ryker spread her hands and hovered her palms inches from my skin, then moved around my head, down my back, out, and up my arms.

"I had a reiki massage like this once," I muttered. "It was about this satisfying."

"Another ex?" Ryker asked.

I grinned. "Maybe." He'd been a bouncer who did reiki massages on the side. When it turned out he was more hands-off than on, my libido became more off than on.

When she came back around to my front, her hands dropped to her side. She walked over to the burned symbols over my trashed stove. Her voice was incredulous. "This was the result of a potion spell?"

"Afraid so." I scratched my head. "I added one too many pinches of this and that."

"Marigold modified a guidance spell."

"I love to cook," I remarked casually, a shrug punctuating my words. "But I was never much good at following recipes."

"She's very talented," Carver said. "She has a rare talent for intuitive witchcraft."

"I see." Ryker's eyes were hooded as she cast her gaze on me once again. "Can I see your hand and the stone?"

I withdrew both from my pocket. I held my hand out with the token in my palm.

"Carver says that your djinn called this his token?"

I nodded. "He did."

She blinked. "He must care for you deeply." Hovering her palm over mine, she asked, "May I?"

I nodded, thinking I was in for some more reiki crap, but she snatched the rock up.

"Hey," I protested.

Ryker held the stone up, examining it like she was prepping for a pop quiz. "Interesting," she said.

"Why is it interesting?" I asked.

She glanced down at my hand. "The binding was on this stone before the spell?"

"Binding?"

"The symbols."

"Oh, yes. Along with the red lines on my palm." My gaze met hers. "Do you know what it means or why it would transfer from the token to my hand?"

"The magic that I saw in your aura belongs to your ifrit."

I had a sinking feeling in my stomach that I knew the answer. "I absorbed his soul, didn't I?"

Ryker nodded. "I am certain you did. You are now the *sebtusiptu* for your Zev."

"Oh, no." My lower back suddenly gave on me, and my knees went jelly. I sat down at the table so I wouldn't collapse. "What does this mean for Zev? For that matter, for me?"

"It means you're in great danger, Marigold." Ryker didn't sugarcoat her words. "No one can know, or you will be vulnerable to anyone seeking to control a djinn."

I pivoted my gaze to my notes on the table. "Like the hunter?"

"The hunter?"

I gave Ryker a hard look. "Is it possible for Zev to communicate with me now that I've absorbed a piece of his soul?"

"Maybe. It's hard to penetrate a mind. Especially one that's alert."

"What about a sleeping one?" I dragged the paper across the table until it was in front of me. "I had a dream about Zev last night. It happens a lot, but he gave me a message this time."

Ryker held out her hand. "Show me."

"Do you know who the hunter is?"

"I don't," she said, taking my dream note. "But I've heard of the hunter. Their identity is one of the best-kept secrets in our world. They procure goods for the highest bidder, and they don't care if there is collateral damage."

"The supernatural dark web," Michael said. "At least that's what it sounds like."

Ryker nodded. "That's exactly what it is."

Her fear amped up my own, but I wouldn't turn my back on Zev. He was in trouble, and I was his only life-line. "Zev said to find the hunter. If that's what he wants me to do, then that's what I'll do. How do I contact this hunter person?"

"I will tell you on one condition," Ryker said.

"And what's that?"

"You allow me to join you on this journey."

"That sounds workable." The more, the merrier, as far as I was concerned.

"And you agree to listen to my council if I feel like you are going down a too dangerous path."

I nodded solemnly. "I agree to listen." However, I didn't agree to abide by her council.

"That's all I can ask." Ryker returned my stone. "Pack for a couple of days travel. We'll leave tonight."

"Where too?"

"Mexico," she stated. "We can take my plane."

"You have a plane?" Michael asked incredulously.

"A small Cessna," Ryker replied with a satisfied smile. "It's my baby."

"I'm going home to pack." My nephew headed toward the front door.

I firmly said, "You're not coming, Michael."

He whipped around and pinned me with a glare. "The hell I'm not. I'm not a kid anymore."

"I'll go," Rowan volunteered. "I can call the hospital and have someone cover my days this week—"

"Sorry." Ryker held up her hand to stop him. "My plane has enough room for only three people and some light packing. The third seat goes to Carver if he wants it."

"It's too dangerous," I warned him. "I don't know what I'd do if you got hurt. Besides, this isn't your problem. It's mine, and I should be the one to deal with it."

Carver sighed. "I'm going," he said. "Burdens are meant to be shared. I'm going, and that's the end of it."

I hoped it wasn't the beginning of the end.

Chapter Six

Ryker's vague directions about our destination in Mexico had turned packing a single bag into a Herculean effort. This wasn't a leisure trip. It was a desperate mission to find Zev and bring him home. I had packed with the grim awareness that we might confront thorny situations—literally and figuratively. Shirts of varying sleeve lengths, maxi skirts for versatility, a fancy dress for potential upscale scenarios, shorts for sandy shores, and long pants for the dreaded jungle. Oh, how I prayed we wouldn't end up in that godforsaken jungle.

Tossing in those rarely worn running shoes Rose had given me a couple of years ago for my birthday, a pair of sandals, ballet flats, and even heels, I prepared for every eventuality, no matter how improbable. As for hair and skincare essentials? Let's just say I had to make some tough choices. I packed a small backpack to use as a purse for a little extra room.

On one hand, I was sorry that Michael and Rowan couldn't come along, but on the other, this adventure could turn deadly fast. I wanted my brother and nephew away from that kind of danger. Besides, I'd told Iris I'd look out for Michael, and taking him out of the country to confront someone on the supernatural dark web wouldn't get me the Aunt of the Year award.

I truly believed Zev was in trouble. I'd absorbed a piece of him into my hand, and I was his only lifeline back to safety and freedom—at least, that's what I kept telling myself. I was glad Carver had agreed to come along. I needed to find this hunter, and the only way to do that was to let a stranger take the lead. Having a friendly face and someone I could trust along for this wild ride was the only thing keeping me sane.

We'd parked under the cover of trees near a long, narrow runway in the middle of a grassy field. As we trudged across, a loud, squabbling flock of geese migrating north cut through the isolated silence, reminding me that this flight was going to be as illegal as hell and off the radar. What if we ran into other birds while flying south as they were traveling north? I'd seen shows about birds hitting propellers and taking down small aircraft, and Ryker's white Cessna was certainly small.

The moon hung low in the Arkansas sky, its beams of silver and blue shining over the patchy grass. The plane sat squat and unassuming against the rural landscape, its metal exterior gleaming dully in the glowing light. A chilly breeze cut through the air, carrying the faint scent of impending rain. I rubbed my arms, grateful for the fleece sweater I'd worn.

Ryker stepped out from behind the plane wearing a black leather jacket that reminded me of Zev's. She waved. "Throw your bags in the cargo hold."

"Which side?" I asked.

"Either," she pointed to the rear of the plane. "There are doors on both sides. I hope you packed light. I'm pushing the weight limit with the three of us and luggage. It wouldn't normally be a big deal," she explained, "but I have some extra gear that I have to bring along, and let's just say, if something has to be thrown out of the plane at fifteen thousand feet, it won't be my stuff."

"Gotcha." I stuffed my bag into the cargo hold, a surge of anxiety sweeping through me like a chill wind. My hand lingered on the hull of the plane as doubts about the mission swirled around in my head.

Was this crazy? Carver trusted Ryker, but I didn't. She was a stranger, and I was putting myself at her mercy. Would this trip even lead to Zev? Was he really lost in the labyrinth of Mexico's supernatural underbelly? No matter how remote the possibility, I had to take the chance. I knew in my heart he'd do the same for me. Gah. The mere possibility of never seeing him again clawed at my insides. And who or what was this hunter? What did he have to do to earn the enigmatic title?

Was I going through with this? Yes.

Was I crazy? Again, yes.

Since Iris's transformation into a tru-craft witch, I'd

seen my fair share of paranormal creatures. I'd even killed a seven-foot foul-mouthed satyr who was trying to steal the pixie king's mate and kill my sister in the process. I knew Iris and the rest of my family worried about me and my attraction to dangerous men, but I could admit if only to myself, that I was the one who had a problem with violence. Nothing jazzed me quite like a good fight. Killing, though, that had been a whole 'nother story.

Even so, I had no regrets when it came to bashing that asshole's horny head in. What would the hunter be? A dragon dripping in merciless greed? Maybe a werewolf stalking the night with feral hunger? Or perhaps a vampire, elegant yet deadly and cruel? I would blow up that bridge after I crossed it. I thought knowing where we were going would make me feel better. I was seriously wrong.

"Where are you taking us, and how much room will there be to land?" The strip we were on stretched the length of a football field.

"If it comes down to it, I can land this baby with less than five hundred feet of clearing." Ryker snorted. "Not that I'll need it. As to the where, we're headed to Isla de Altamura, a private island in the Sea of Cortes. It's off the coast on the Pacific side near Sinaloa. Any more questions?" She opened the passenger door and dropped down some fold-out stairs. "Excellent. After you."

As I climbed up the steps, I paused at the top. "Wait a minute, what do you mean you won't need it? What won't you need?"

"A runway." Ryker's nonchalance was disturbing as she patted me on the back and ushered me inside the cabin. She grinned mischievously and said, "I don't plan to land."

I buckled into my seat, my gut gurgling with excitement and fear. "What do you mean?"

She settled into the cockpit and turned in her seat. Her dark eyes swirled with intensity. "It's hard to explain." She gestured at Carver, whose nose was in his phone. "Get yourself strapped in. There's a storm brewing out there, and it's going to be a bumpy ride."

Carver looked up, confusion evident. "Altamura is an uninhabited sandbar."

"Sure," Ryker acknowledged. "In this plane."

"In this plane? You mean the one we're sitting in?" I asked.

"No," the djinn expert replied. "The one we live in. This plane of existence is not the one we're staying on."

I was more befuddled than ever. Shit had the potential to go very south. "And what plane are we going to?"

"Natheria in the Aetherrelm." She smiled and started flicking buttons on her console. My gut clenched as lights flickered on the dash. "Don't worry. I've made this flight dozens of times. I'll get you there, no problem."

"Isn't the Aetherrelm fae land?" Carver asked.

"Ah," she said. "You remember the stories I used to tell you."

"I do." He shifted uncomfortably as he tightened his seat belt. "But I wasn't sure Aetherrelm actually existed."

"Surprise," Ryker said. "It's all real, baby." The plane sputtered and then roared to life. "Here we go."

"Do we have enough gas to get over the Pacific?" I wasn't sure what kind of mileage this Cessna got, but I dated an aerial stunt pilot when I was thirty, and his plane always seemed low on fuel.

"That's why my *Mystara* is a wee bit heavy. I've modified her with extra fuel space and ... other items."

"Miss Tara?" I said loudly so she could hear me.

"Mystara," she answered as we started our taxi down the runway. "M-Y-S-T-A-R-A." The noise inside the plane grew louder as she increased our speed.

"Cool-cool." I anxiously clutched my backpack on my lap. My phone rang as the front pocket on my pack began to vibrate. Startled, I scrambled to retrieve it. "I'm so sorry," I yelled up to Ryker. "I forgot to turn it off." When I saw the lit-up screen, my heart leaped in my chest. "Oh, hell. It's Iris!" She was finally calling me back. I glanced back and forth between the screen and the cockpit. What would happen if I answered?

"Go ahead," Ryker shouted back. "But you might want to use some headphones."

Luckily, I'd packed my noise-canceling pair in my pack. I quickly answered the phone and bellowed, "Hold on!" to my sister. "Don't hang up." I got my headphones turned on and covered my ears.

They instantly connected to my phone via Bluetooth, and I heard Iris say, "What in the world are you doing? Why does it sound like you're riding a lawnmower?"

"I'm on a plane," I replied. "A very loud one." Although, the headphones provided some sweet relief from the loud noise. "Where have you been? Why haven't you called me back?"

"Bad reception here," she explained. It wasn't the first time she'd used the excuse, but I was starting to have doubts about their so-called vacation.

I couldn't worry what Iris was or wasn't up to at this moment. I had my own problem that needed solving. "When did you last speak to Zev?"

"Oh, Marigold. Not this again," Iris lamented. "Zev is good. He'll return when he's ready."

"He told you this?"

"Yes," she reiterated.

"When? And did you speak to him or was it a text?"

"I...he texted," she said hesitantly. "Does it matter?"

"When was the last time?"

"Three weeks ago." There was a pause on her end. "I have my messages up now. Here. A little less than three weeks ago, I texted him for my monthly check-in, and he wrote back. *I'm fine. Do not worry for me. I'll return when I am ready.*" Another pause. "Look, I can text him again if that would make you feel better."

My head slammed back, and my stomach lurched as we lifted off the ground. "Whoa," I sputtered.

"No?" Iris asked.

"*Yes.* Text him." I needed her to ask him something that only Zev would know. If it wasn't Zev, the person on the other end of his phone would get it wrong. There was a spattering of freckles on my inner left thigh that Zev had said reminded him of the constellation Andromeda. He's spent a lot of time studying that star system and the surrounding area. I knew the story of Andromeda from my study of women in Greek Mythology. She'd been sacrificed by her mother and rescued by Perseus, who later became her husband. I'd told Zev on several occasions that if I'd been tied to that rock, fated to die at the hands of a sea monster, I would've found a way to save myself.

He laughed and said, "Of that, I have no uncertainty. You would've been a great hero—perhaps the greatest of all time. There would be tomes devoted to you and your exploits."

The plane began to shake, and I clutched the armrest with my free hand. "Ask him if he wants me to find a new home for Andromeda?"

"Who's Andromeda?"

"Just ask."

"Okay, hold on."

Carver's hand rested on mine. I turned my palm, and our fingers intertwined. I cast my gaze in his direction, and his eyes were firmly shut. The turbulence was easing up as we flew higher out of the cloudy weather.

"He says he doesn't care what you do with the animal." My sister made a disgusted noise. "It can go to the pound."

"It's not him." I didn't know whether to be horrified or relieved. I shot for somewhere in the middle.

"Andromeda is not a cat, and the only pound Zev would want me to take it is to pound-town with him."

"Ew!" Iris exclaimed. "And what do you mean it's not him?"

"Zev is being held against his will. Whoever has him is the one texting you."

"You're.....eak..up. I...half...that," I heard, then the phone dinged, and the call was dropped.

"Damn it!" I tried to call her back, but I had no bars. "I lost her!" I shouted to Ryker.

"Sorry," she quipped. "You'll just have to wait until we pass over another cell tower."

In the interim, I typed out a phone message for Iris detailing everything that had happened between yesterday and today. It would send when we were once again in cell range. I assured her Michael was safe at home and that Rowan would keep an eye out for the kid. I finished my text with, *I love you. Thank you for inviting me into your world and giving me the best time of my midlife. I thought my adventures were over, and I'm so happy to learn they've just begun. P.S. whatever you're up to in Ireland, please keep yourself safe.*

"It's going to be a long flight," Ryker informed us. "Try and get some sleep. Natheria isn't a place you want to be without a clear head."

As the plane cut through the sky, I leaned back against the seat and closed my eyes. I braced for whatever awaited us in Natheria. Zev had been the closest I'd ever gotten to happily ever after, and even if we couldn't be together, that didn't mean I wouldn't move mountains...or in this case, planes of existence to find him. I took my hand back from Carver and rubbed Zev's symbols embedded in my palm.

I'm coming for you, Perseus, I thought. And god help any monsters who tried to get in my way.

Chapter Seven

Strong arms wrapped me from behind in a loving embrace, and I sank against the warmth of the familiar body. I rested my head on Zev's shoulder, reaching to thread my fingers through his hair as he kissed my neck. A rush of heat pooled in my belly and pulsated as it grew.

I turned and kissed him, exaltation coursing through me as his hands slid down my back and he cupped my derriere. "I have missed this ass."

I grinned. "Don't stay away so long, and there won't be anything to miss."

"You're correct." He leaned me back, kissing my neck and then my collarbone. "I will put you in a bottle and carry you with me wherever I go."

I tilted my head to look at him. "Is that a genie joke?" He looked slightly distorted, as if I were seeing him through an oiled lens. I rubbed my eyes to clear them.

There was a flashing light. It changed colors in a repeating pattern: blue, yellow, green, yellow, yellow, blue, and red.

"What is this?" I tried to let go of him, but he kept a firm hold of me. "Zev?"

"Do not come for me," he whispered.

"It's too late for that."

Flames flickered in his pupils as he narrowed his gaze on me. "There is nothing you can do for me, Marigold. Not now." He lifted my hand, the one with the symbol. "The danger is too great. You are marked as mine, which places you in grave danger."

"Mark or no mark." I laid my hand over his heart. "I have always been yours."

"You are a sentimental woman."

"You're just now figuring that out?"

He chuckled, his tone low and sexy. "Please, libbu ša. Turn back before it's too late."

The flashing light was getting brighter and faster. "What is that?"

"It's a trap," he said. "We are done, you and I. This is over. Do not come."

A surge of rage burned through me. How fucking dare he? "It's not over," I seethed. "We're not through until you tell me face to face."

"We are face to face."

"The hell we are." My brain was working overtime to make sense of the situation. I scanned the area surrounding us. A giant teddy bear with a yellow bow tied around its neck sat in an oversized rocking chair. A silver

bow and arrow floated against what seemed like a black void. "I'm coming."

"No," he countered firmly. "You are not."

"Yes!" I roared in his face. "I am."

"Stubborn woman." He shook his head. "You are on fire."

"Yeah, I am," I crowed. "And I'm going to ride the flames to you."

He shook his head. "It's not a metaphor. You are on fire. Wake up, Marigold."

"Marigold!" Carver shouted, stirring me from the dream. "Wake the hell up!"

"There's a fire extinguisher by the door," Ryker shouted.

Dazedly, I looked around, unable to move for a moment. The cabin was filled with smoke and flames. "What...what's going on?"

"You shouted something about riding a flame, and then fire shot from your hands and engulfed your entire body." He held the fire extinguisher in his hands. "Turn your head and hold your breath."

I inhaled deeply and held my breath as I looked away, my eyes clamped shut. As surprising as waking up on fire was, getting hit by a blast of high-pressure powder was worse. The shock of cold hitting my skin was like an icy arctic wind. Even with my head turned, the fine powder coated my face. Trying to shield my face didn't help. The slick, powdery substance had coated my hands. I struggled to hold my breath as panic fueled by the disorienting chaos filled me.

And then, as suddenly as it had begun, the onslaught ceased. Carver and Ryker were coughing as the dusty cloud hung in the air.

No longer able to hold my breath, I blew it out noisily and then sucked in a harsh inhalation. "What in the actual-actual?" I rasped out. I tried to get out of my seat, but the seatbelt held me in place.

"Don't get up," Carver instructed. "I need to check your burns."

"Burns?" I didn't feel the tell-tale signs. No searing agony. I stretched my arms out in front of me. No blisters. No redness. Even my hairs were unsinged. How was this possible? "I'm fine." The melted plastic on the armrests, scorch marks on the ceiling, and the heavy scent of smoke were the only casualties of my sudden spontaneous combustion.

"I heard Ryker shouting, and then I felt the intense heat." He held up his right arm. While I didn't have any marks, Carver hadn't been so lucky. The outside of his right forearm looked like a bad sunburn, complete with tiny blisters.

"I did that?"

"It's okay. It looked worse before. I heal quickly, thanks to my sylph side." He finished his cursory exam of me. "You're right. You're completely unscathed." He grimaced. "Other than your wardrobe."

My skirt, shirt, and shoes had felt the full force of the

fire and had been reduced to mostly char and ash. Unfortunately, my underwear had taken a hit as well, and my right boob was hanging out for all the world—at least the world inside the plane—to see. I crossed my arms over my chest. "Fucking hell."

"There's a blanket behind the seats," Ryker yelled. "I'm going to make an emergency landing! Hold on to your knickers." She gestured at me with a flick of her wrist. "Or whatever you got left to hold on to."

Smart ass. Carver retrieved the blanket, and I wrapped it around me. With my eyes squeezed shut and my hands covering the back of my neck, all I could think about was those stupid nuclear drills we did in elementary. The Cold War was ending, but that hadn't stopped the Southill Village school district from running "duck and cover" drills once a quarter. We'd all get under our desks, put our hands over our heads, and our heads on our knees. Dahlia used to joke that the position made it easier to kiss our asses goodbye because if nuclear bombs were dropped on Southill, a whole stack of desks couldn't save us. I had been scared then, and I was afraid now. But it was the kind of scary that got my blood pumping with energy.

I clenched my fists as the nose of the plane dipped in a steep decline. "It's going to be close!" Ryker shouted. "Brace yourselves for a rough landing."

Carver took my hand, and I let him—not because I needed the comfort but because I thought he did. "We're going to be okay," he said.

I ventured a look out the window. The clear moonlit sky highlighted towering trees and a winding river as we dropped closer to the ground. I saw a narrow clearing become more distinct against the verdant backdrop.

My back stiffened. "That's not where we're landing, are we?"

The plane's jarring as the wheels contacted the uneven surface answered my question. The cabin's shake had me clutching the burnt armrests. My heart pounded so hard I could hear it over the engine's roar as Ryker made a series of deft maneuvers before bringing the Cessna to a halt. She began flipping switches, and the engine shut down.

"Get out," Ryker ordered. "Both of you."

"But why?" I asked, confused.

"I can smell gas, and I don't want to take a chance that you're going to ignite again before I can assess the damage."

"Oh." I winced involuntarily. "Sorry." I was still confused by what was happening.

Was this still part of a dream? Had I really exploded into flames? There would be time to process after exiting the aircraft. I grabbed for my backpack, pleased to see it was scorched but intact, and followed Carver out of the passenger door. He helped me down since I was holding onto the blanket for dear life.

The humid air was thick with the scent of damp earth and foliage. The native birds called their outrage at our disruption of their environment. It would've sounded like a cacophony of noises to most people, but I heard, "Alert. Danger. Intruder!" in their cries.

"We won't be staying long," I called back to them. "Just a brief stop to get our shit together." I snorted at the thought. When was the last time I had my shit together?

"Here," Carver said. He handed me my bag. He'd retrieved it from the back of the plane. "I thought you'd like a change of clothes."

I shot him a thankful glance, then eagerly took it from him. I'd packed wipes in my backpack, so I dug those out first. "Can you hold the blanket up for me while I get cleaned and changed?"

"Absolutely," he said.

Carver took the offered blanket and held it up with his head turned away.

I smiled. I wasn't sure what kind of privacy I had in the middle of the jungle or wherever we were, but the illusion of privacy felt like everything. "Where do you think we landed?"

"Somewhere in Sinaloa," he answered. "Ryker announced it when we crossed into the state." He was silent for a moment before adding, "That's when you went up in flames. What happened?"

"Your guess is as good as mine." I used the wet wipe to clean the extinguisher dust from my face and neck. "One second, I was sleeping and dreaming, then the next, I'm waking up on fire."

"Dreaming?" he asked. "About Zev again?"

I shifted my gaze to Carver. "Yes, I was." The fire had

knocked the dream from my thoughts. I did some mental gymnastics to remember what had taken place. I warmed as I remembered his lips against the skin of my neck and the feel of his hands on my body. But we'd talked as well. A sinking feeling came over me. "He warned me not to come. He said it's dangerous for me now that I'm marked."

I left out the whole and marked as mine. It seemed a little archaic for someone who taught women's studies for a living to get excited about a man claiming her. It was barbaric but also thrilling. Granted, had it been any other man but Zev, I would have kneed them in the balls hard enough for them to taste future generations at the back of their throat. Even so, mark or no mark, I was my own woman and would make my own decisions. If Zev thought he could dissuade me from looking for him, he was sorely mistaken.

"I see," Carver said. "Did he say anything else?"

He'd told me we were done. I'd been so angry at his words. Furious. A bright glow made me look down. "Damn it," I hissed. I shook my flaming hand. Again, I didn't feel any pain...or hot for that matter. The blanket, however, had caught on fire. I knocked it down and out of Carver's hands.

"What the hell?" He stared at my hands as the flame died out. "This is new."

"Very," I agreed, rubbing my palms against my naked thighs.

The birds, along with some warbling coyotes,

sounded the alarm. "Humans," they said. "Danger. Danger. Stay away."

"Yes," I signaled with a wave. We're humans. Sort of." I muttered the last part. Ryker was a half-djinn, Carver was a half-sylph, and I was a half-giant, and whatever else was going on with me.

I fished my clothes out of the bag, put on new underwear and a bra, then chose long pants, a long-sleeved shirt, and tennis shoes. I had a dozen hair ties shoved inside my backpack and used one to tie my hair into a loose bun.

"Coming. Coming now," a bird squelched.

"We're going," I told him. "Soon."

"Who are you talking to?" Carver asked.

"The native fauna." I pointed to the trees. A large, colorful toucan was sitting on a low branch at the edge. "There's one of them. They don't like us being here."

In the distance, I heard the sound of a truck engine.

"Coming!" the bird squawked again. "Run!"

"That's not good."

"What's not good?" Carver asked.

"I hear a truck coming, and the bird says to run."

Ryker came out of the plane, wiping off a tool and shaking her head. "The bird's not wrong, but we're not going anywhere. Your little fire fried the sensors on the fuel tank. Mystara's not safe to fly."

"Is it less safe than staying here?"

The purple-haired half-djinn sighed. "Unfortunately, neither option is safe. I'm sure the emergency landing was picked up by someone in the local cartel. They're probably on their way to see if the plane is full of contraband they can steal. And if there isn't, they'll try to kidnap or kill us." She threw a couple of duffels onto the ground, then raised the stairs and closed the door. "I have some tamper spells on the plane that'll keep them out of her or from moving her until I can get back with the parts I need to get her back in the air, but right now, we need to move."

"Move where?"

"Toward the coast," she answered. "We can get a boat to Natheria from there."

I couldn't keep the appalled tone from my voice. "How far will we be walking?"

Ryker shrugged and pulled both duffels over her shoulders. "About twelve miles." She nodded toward some unknown location in the distance. "Grab your gear. It's going to be a hike." She gave me a pointed look. "Unless you want to take your chances with the cartel."

"What if we get lost?" I protested, already picking up my stuff and preparing to go. "Navigating through a forest of trees isn't easy."

"You know what's easy?" Ryker asked. "Dying."

"Been there, done that, got the t-shirt," I countered.

Ryker chuckled, then clapped me on the back. She gestured to the toucan. "Lucky for us, we have a trail guide who can talk to the locals."

Chapter Eight

THE PRIMAL BEAUTY OF THE FOREST, ITS VIBRANT hues and lush foliage lost its charm once the gnats and mosquitos started swarming around.

"Can't you tell them to buzz off," Ryker joked.

Carver chuckled but didn't comment.

"I can talk to animals, not bugs." Despite the remote location and the challenges ahead, I was exhilarated. Which meant I probably needed therapy and lots of it. The toucan, whose name wasn't Sam—it was Lo-kwahk— had been scouting ahead for us, then coming back to report when all was clear. Some other forest animals followed us at a safe distance, curious about the woman who could understand their language and her companions.

We'd had snakes, a white-tailed deer, some smaller birds, and a cute little coati that reminded me of a skinny raccoon with the tail of a cat and a tiny piggy snout at the end of its nose. The coati stayed with us long after we left the other animals' territories.

I glanced over a few times, giving the small, sleek creature a nod and a smile. Every time, it would duck behind a tree or into a bush. For all its fear, it didn't stop following us. After a couple of hours, I was sweaty, tired, hungry, and thirsty. On top of that, my thighs and low back were in pain.

"Can we stop for a few minutes?" I was exhausted. Maybe I should've taken Rose up on her offer to get me a guest pass for her gym. Of course, hindsight was twenty-twenty. I couldn't have known at the time that I'd be hiking miles and miles through a dense forest in Mexico. "I need a break."

Ryker dropped her packs. "We'll take five and hydrate."

"And carb load," I added hopefully. The one thing I hadn't packed for was getting stranded in the middle of nowhere without food.

"I have protein bars," Carver said. "Vanilla or maple pecan?"

"Ooo. Maple pecan, please." I set my bag down and used it as a seat to keep me off the forest floor. "I don't suppose you brought your magic supplies?" I asked Carver. "I'd pay good money for a bug-be-gone potion."

He shook his head. "I brought some items, but not my potion supplies."

"I wish someone would've thought of bug spray," I grumbled.

"Who knew you'd turn into a fireball and we'd end up trekking through a forest?" Ryker questioned. "Not me, that's for sure."

I couldn't tell if she was being sarcastic. I took the protein bar Carver handed me and ripped open the package like a marooned sailor who'd found his first coconut. "Mmmmm," I hummed as I chewed the first sweet bit. Oh, man, it smelled so good—like pancakes with maple syrup and toasted pecans. As hungry as I was, it tasted like a meal fit for a queen. "So good," I said through a mouthful. "Thank heavens we don't have to eat bugs."

Ryker swatted at the ones flying in front of her face. "There's plenty around if it comes down to it." She'd taken one of the protein bars as well. She had some bottled water in her bag and passed it around. "Drink up. We still have a way to go and need to stay hydrated."

"Were you a Girl Scout or something?" I asked.

"I was," she said. "I was a Daisy, Brownie, Junior, and Cadette. I quit before I hit senior rank."

"How come?" I was fascinated. This punk rock chick in front of me didn't seem like the type to join the scouts. "What made you stop?"

"My mom got sick when I was thirteen. I was all she had, so I spent the next four years helping to take care of her until she died." She said it so casually I almost choked on my food. "Not a lot of time for scouts when that happens."

"Damn." I had so much sympathy for Ryker. I'd been an adult when my mother died. Grace Everlee was a queen among mothers. I'd gotten lucky when she had chosen me to be her daughter. Her death had been devastating for all of us. I couldn't even imagine what it would've been like to suffer through it as a young teenager, let alone do it alone. My sisters, brother and I had all rallied around each other, checking in and ensuring we had whatever support we needed. On top of that, we shared the responsibility of looking out for Dad. "I'm so sorry, Ryker. It must've been awful to be alone through all that."

"It was a long time ago." She shrugged and took another bite. "Sometimes it feels like another life."

"Wasn't she from Indonesia?" Carver asked before taking a swig of water. Carver, like me, was built more for finding the comfiest spot on the couch than running a marathon. "I think I remember you telling me she'd been a refugee when she came to the United States."

"That's right," she said with a slight smile. "Mama was of Chinese descent. In the sixties, the regime in Indonesia blamed the ethnic Chinese for a failed coup attempt. After, they slaughtered over half a million Chinese Indonesians. They took land indiscriminately and imprisoned those who were spared. My mother, a true beauty, had been in hiding when a young, handsome Indonesian man found her and helped her escape to

America. She never saw him again." She gave me a sly look. "But I did. It turned out he wasn't Indonesian at all. He was a marid djinn."

I got goosebumps. "Your father?"

Ryker nodded. "I think he'd cared for my mother as much as a djinn can." She gave me a meaningful look. "Are you sure you want to continue this pursuit of the ifrit? Even if we find him, I am not sure the ending will be the one you want."

"If the ending finds him safe and free, I'll call it a win."

"You're an unusual woman, Marigold." She blinked, her wide eyes curious. Suddenly, she narrowed her gaze. "Would you like to know more about the ifrit Za'fir of Mesopotamia?"

"You've heard of Zev?"

"You can't call yourself a djinnologist and not know who the most prominent working djinns are. Especially the ones who have fought to free many enslaved djinns." She finished the last bite of her energy bar. "Including my father."

I whipped my gaze to Carver. "Did you know this?"

He shook his head. "It's the first I've heard about it."

"It's the reason I agreed to come in the first place." She gave Carver a lopsided smile. "Our friendship aside, I wanted to meet the man who saved my father from an eternity of slavery and, in turn, my mother from certain death at the hands of soldiers or worse. A wealthy sultan had trapped my father for over a thousand years. Forced to do his master's bidding. Zev freed him."

My brow furrowed. "How?"

"By killing the sultan."

"That's anticlimactic."

Carver snorted a laugh, then groaned. "I shot water out my nose."

I shook my head and giggled. "I only meant that it seems like a pretty easy solution for someone trapped for a thousand-plus years." My brows raised as I realized what I said. A thousand-plus years. How could the sultan live that long?"

Ryker grinned, which made her look even younger. "Now you see. This man had bargained for immortality. Taking that from him was no easy feat."

"Wait a minute." I scooted forward, my bag shifting under my weight. Zev once told me that there are certain wishes djinns can't grant. Immortality was one of them. How'd the sultan manage to make it happen?"

"The sultan, a cunning man, was granted the traditional three wishes. One was that my father would serve as his closest most true advisor and defender for the rest of his life—for a djinn, not a life sentence. Most humans, especially in the late seventeen hundreds, had shorter life spans. However, the sultan's second wish was to live as long as my father lived."

"Wow. Immortality loophole. Twisted," I said. "Why didn't your father let him age without dying? I'm sure once the sultan turned into a dried husk of a man, he'd have begged to get out of the wish."

"Ah." Ryker held up a finger. "The sultan's third wish was to stay young in body and mind."

"So he got to stay young in the process."

"Yep." Ryker took another drink of water and gestured for us to do the same.

"This guy thought of everything," Carver said, swatting at a bug on his face.

"No doubt." I tilted my head to Ryker. "So, how did Zev save him then?"

"As the sultan's truest and most trusted advisor and defender, my father couldn't allow any harm to come to the sultan as long as it was in his power to prevent it. So, Zev prevented it. He put my father in a bottle, capped it, and sealed it with his fire."

"The old djinn jar trick," I muttered. "I know it well." After all, it was the reason Zev embraced his fire again.

"Then what happened? The guy was still basically immortal."

"But immortality doesn't grant freedom from pain and agony."

Carver shook his head. "Zev tortured him."

"And then some." Ryker laughed as if she'd been there. "After your Zev sawed off the sultan's arms with a dull knife, he gave the sultan one wish. This wish would nullify the ones he bargained for with my father. "You can live, but I will torture you until you pray for death, he

93

told the man, or you can wish for me to stop torturing you, and I will simply kill you now. What shall it be?"

I whistled. "A real dilemma."

"The man chose to stop the torture."

"I bet he did." Carver blew out a breath. "What happened after?"

"With the sultan dead, there was nothing left of him to defend. Za'fir let him out of the bottle and became his new master."

I pressed my fingers to my lips. "Okay, another plot twist."

"Not to worry. Zev's three wishes were that my father would aid the helpless, when possible, find a purpose for his long life, and he would never again go back in the bottle. Effectively, he freed my father for eternity."

Damn it. Just when I thought I couldn't love the man more. My heart did a jumping jack. "That's my guy."

"He cut limbs off a guy," Carver said. "Don't get all romantic about it."

"Some girls like flowers." I gave him a feral grin. "Some like stems."

Ryker belly laughed for nearly an entire minute. When she settled, she said, "Five minutes are up. We better get moving."

The coati following us poked its head from behind a tree. "Hello, beautiful lady. I am Racón."

"Oh my." I tucked my chin. "Hello, Racón. Can I help you with something?"

"I help you, pretty lady."

"You want to help me?" I got up from the ground. "How would you like to help me?"

"Do you understand anything that rodent is saying to her?" Ryker asked Carver as she closed her duffel.

"Nope," he replied. "She'll fill us in when she's finished."

"Here." Racón held out a bunch of leaves in his clawed paw.

"Leaves for me?" I took them and then wrinkled my nose at their earthy but also astringent odor. "You shouldn't have."

"Bug away," he chittered. "Pretty lady. No bites. No bother."

I looked at Carver. "Racón the coati says these leaves will keep the bugs away."

"Really?" he crossed over to me and took one of the leaf branches from me. He started to laugh.

"What's so funny?

"Do you know what this is?"

"Please don't tell me it's something awful like poison ivy." I held the leaves away from my body.

Carver shook his head. "It's Mexican Marigold." He laughed again. "The coati brought Mexican Marigold to an American Marigold."

"Ha ha." After a quick roll of my eyes, I laughed. "And it will keep the bugs away?"

"Yep," Carver said. "And I can use it to create a repel spell to keep the bugs far away."

"I'll take some of that," Ryker told him.

The toucan began to grunt and snort. "In the trees. Coming. Coming. Must go. Come." The large bird flew off in the direction it wanted us to follow.

I rubbed the leaves on my shirt and then handed them to Carver. "We're going to need that potion on the go," I told Ryker and him. "Company is closing in from behind."

Chapter Nine

THESE SHOES MIGHT BE BUILT FOR RUNNING, BUT I wasn't. The third time I tripped, it was over protruding roots and I twisted my knee. With a squelch of pain, I staggered, seeking support against a smooth-barked tree. Carver and Ryker slowed their pace to help me. Damn it, I was going to get us all killed if I couldn't pull myself together. Iris would've dispatched the people tracking us with hardly any effort. Keir and Luanne, both druids, were well-versed in hand-to-hand combat, and even Linda the gnome could kick some serious ass. What in the world did I think I was going to do to save Zev? I could barely breathe right now, let alone keep myself out of trouble.

"Come on," Ryker urged. "We have to keep moving."

Voices echoed in the distance behind us. The men weren't going to give up. They would've assumed whoever had been on the plane was now on foot. Their inability to breach the aircraft would've fueled their drive to find the strangers who had flown into their territory.

I worked to slow my breathing, then spoke quietly but concisely. "I can't move this fast. I'm an out-of-shape middle-aged woman. I'm good with long walks and the occasional sprint, but long-distance running is not going to happen."

Racón was still paralleling us as we headed to the coast. "Here," he said. "Hide. Hide."

I shook my head. "We can't hide." I glanced from the small animal to Carver and Ryker. "Right?"

Ryker looked at me worriedly. "I'm not sure we have any options at this point. They are closing in on us fast. We still have a few miles to travel before we hit the coast. If we can't shake them, hiding until they give up might be the best option. Does your friend know a place?"

I gazed back at Racón. "Where?" I asked him.

"Cave. Nearby." He chirped and woofed as he bounded away. "Follow me."

"He wants us to follow him to a cave."

Ryker grunted as she followed the coati's path. "This isn't how I thought this night was going to go."

"What? Your plans don't always go off the rails?" I inquired as I hobbled after.

"Not usually," she admitted. "I don't start a job until I've had time to prepare for all eventualities. This one was a little last minute."

"All because of Zev?"

"You got it on the first go," Ryker recounted, her voice

carrying a mix of determination and regret as she navigated the rugged terrain. "When Carver told me who this was about—that the man who'd saved my father's life was in trouble—I couldn't walk away. I let my emotion cloud my good sense."

I chuckled softly, feeling a kinship with her plight. "Welcome to my world."

The coati led us down a steep incline to a rocky path. "Here," he indicated, his movements quick and purposeful. "Cave. Hide. Bad men not find."

Lava-like rocks and boulders made the trek uneven and hard to navigate. The burgeoning dawn presented both a blessing and a curse. The ground was more visible, but then, so were we. Carrying my bag made the journey more difficult.

Suck it up, buttercup, I told myself. "You're not a princess who needs rescuing. You are the knight in shining armor. So, pull yourself together."

"What?" Carver inquired, glancing over.

"Did I say that out loud?"

"'Fraid so," he confirmed with a grin. "I like it. Come on, Knight. Let's live to fight another day."

Ryker reached the cave first. It was around four feet in height and seven or eight feet wide—not great for a half-giantess. Carver and Ryker were also tall, so the space felt claustrophobia-inducing.

"How far back does this go?" I probed, turning my attention to Racón.

His ringed tail swished back and forth, very cat-like. "To water."

I sought clarification. "To the ocean?"

"Water," Racón reiterated, his words sharp and to the point. "Big water, big waves."

Animals didn't use filler words, so their information was usually succinct and without a lot of description. They didn't have a bunch of synonyms and stuck with concepts like big and small, but I found the descriptors relevant to the animal's size. Coatis were the size of opossums, which meant lots of things were "big" in their estimation. "Big like sky or big like tree."

"Not tall like tree," he clarified. "Wide like clouds, but not big like sky."

Maybe he wasn't talking about the ocean. "Well, futz."

Carver retrieved some of his spelling tools from his bag. Mosquitoes were everywhere, so I understood the necessity to make the bug repellent. We were hidden, so now was as good a time as any. "What did the coati say?" he asked, his gaze shifting between Racón and me.

"There's water at the end of this tunnel. Hold on." I directed my attention back to Racón. "Is the water outside the cave or inside the cave?"

"Inside," the small coati answered.

I nodded. "It's inside."

"Great," Ryker grumbled, swatting at mosquitoes.

"And outside," Racón added, starting to move toward the exit. "Short swim to outside."

"Interesting," I remarked, glancing at my friends and adjusting my bag strap. "If we don't mind getting wet, this might be our way to the coast. Racón says it's a short swim through the inside water to get outside."

We could hear men calling to each other as they looked for us out in the forest. Ryker nodded. "I don't think we have much choice."

I looked at Carver inquisitively as he sorted through his tools.

He brushed his black hair from his face and smiled. "You know I don't mind the water." Holding out a small metal cup, he added, "Smear this on your neck and arms. It'll keep the mosquitoes at bay."

"With pleasure," I accepted, though the aroma was pungent and unpleasant, wrinkling my nose. "Maybe pleasure is a strong word."

"Give me some," Ryker eagerly requested, dipping two fingers into the paste and started to spread it onto her skin. "I'm getting eaten alive in here."

Racón swished his semi-erect tail and began to leave the cave, his footsteps echoing.

"Hey," I called after him, adjusting my bag on my shoulder. "Thank you for your help."

"Gratitude," he replied, turning back briefly. "Big adventure. Story to share with family."

"You're welcome, my friend," I responded, nodding in acknowledgment. "I will share the story of you with my family."

Racón puffed with pride as he exited the cave. I

looked at my companions, adjusting my bag again. "We're on our own now."

With Ryker leading the way, her flashlight cutting through the darkness, we ventured deeper into the cave. The corridor grew narrower the further we traveled. Navigating the cramped space was like threading a needle with yarn. No easy task. The damp air felt heavy around us. Even stooped, I'd knocked my head on several protrusions from the ceiling and scraped my shoulders on the rough walls.

Good news. Carver's repel potion worked. Nothing wanted to be close to us while we wore the stinky paste. Hell, if I could've gotten away from myself, I would've.

With each step, I had to crouch lower, my knees protesting against the strain. Ryker's light illuminated the path ahead, casting eerie shadows that danced on the uneven walls. My heart pounded as the thought of being trapped under a mountain of solid rock triggered my fight-or-flight reflexes.

I forced myself to slow my breathing. Having a panic attack now was only going to make matters worse. We pressed forward, my senses on high alert as every rustle of our clothes and bags amplified the quiet of the cave.

After what felt like an hour of silence, I said, "How much—"

Ryker started, which made me start, and that startled Carver.

An anxious laugh escaped me, echoed by Ryker's chuckle.

"Holy crap on toast," she muttered. "I didn't realize how jumpy I was getting. Whew." A swallow punctuated her words. "What were you saying?"

"How much further do you think it is?" I asked, my nerves still on edge.

Carver's hand found my shoulder. "I can feel the water." His eyes had turned bright blue.

Ryker smiled. "I see you've been exploring your sylph side. Good for you," she said. "I'd give my left tit to have some of my father's djinn juice so I could apparate us out of here."

"I'd give my right one to have the knees of my twenty-year-old self again," I complained. "Or at least a couple of ibuprofens."

My lamenting made both of them laugh again.

"We are a motley crew, aren't we?" I asked.

"The rag-taggiest," Ryker agreed.

"That's the best kind," Carver added as we rounded another bend in the cave corridor. "It's not far. I can feel the water moving below us. It's just up ahead."

The pathway narrowed again and then opened to a large chamber stretched out like a cathedral. The room was filled with intricate formations of stalactites and stalagmites.

The air hung heavy with a faint mustiness as shafts of sunlight filtered through crevices from above. In the heart of the chamber, a pool of water shimmered as Ryker's flashlight skimmed the surface.

"This is it," I said. "We finally made it." I stretched

my arms skyward, rotating my head and moving my low back side to side. "God, it feels good to be able to stand up. You sort of take it for granted, until you walk for two hours in a stooped position." I rolled my shoulders to loosen them. Carver and Ryker stretched as well, but with much less theatrical drama.

The gentle sound of water dripping from stalactite straws made the cavern feel ethereal. Magical.

Carver walked over and dragged his hand through the crystal-clear water. He touched the liquid to his tongue. "It's salty," he said.

"What's that mean for us?" I asked.

"It means this water source is from the ocean."

My insides did a happy dance until I realized I would have to swim through it without knowing how long I'd be underwater. Could I even make the swim? I wasn't sure I could hold my breath for more than a minute. "How far will we have to go?"

Carver took in my worried expression. "I'll go and find out how far and report back." He shed his coat, shirt, and boots. His pale skin glowed in the dim light.

"Get a tan," I teased.

His lean muscles bunched as he swung his arms in an arc. "I'll be back," he said in parting, then dove into the water without hesitation.

"He's pretty spectacular," Ryker said fondly, making me curious.

"He is," I agreed. "Was there something between you two? More than a friendship, I mean."

Ryker grinned as she swept her purple hair away from her face. "Once," she admitted. "He'd turned eighteen, and there was something about tall, dark, and geeky that did it for me."

"It didn't last?"

"Nah." She waved her hand in dismissal. "He liked them short, fair, and geeky." Her grin widened. "Like your brother."

"Oh my gosh," I gushed. "I've thought the same thing. Do you think they're together?"

She winked at me. "If they're not, it's a crime."

"Okay," I told her. "We can officially be friends now."

"But not before?"

"Before, I didn't know you were a Cowan shipper." I tapped my chin. "Or maybe Rarver? Rorvar? Carwan?" I shook my head emphatically. "No, definitely Cowan."

Ryker laughed. "I like you too. You've got a lot of moxie."

"Damn." I chuckled. "You really are a boomer."

Ryker gave me a playful nudge, and we both snickered.

"Can I see your hand?" she asked, sobering the moment.

I held it out to her as my response.

"I've never seen this before."

"The symbol?" I asked.

"No," she replied. "I'm well-versed in ancient Akkadian, the language of the djinn, but I've never seen a *sebtusiptu* inscription in human flesh." She hovered her hand over the top. "Can I touch it?"

"Sure."

She traced the triangles. "Amazing."

"What's amazing?"

"You've imbued yourself with a piece of Za'fir's soul." She gave me an assessing glance. "You must be very powerful."

"My knees and muscles would beg to differ."

She chuckled. "What you've accomplished should be impossible."

"What do you think it means?" I asked her. "You're the djinn expert."

"I think it means we'll have to wait and see." She closed my fingers over my palm. "Until we do, you should keep the symbol hidden. It could be dangerous for you and Zev."

"He said the same thing."

"In your dream?" she inquired.

I nodded. "He said that now that I had his mark, it was too dangerous for me. He's worried they'll use me against him."

"It's a reasonable assumption." She placed a comforting hand on my forearm. "What else did he tell you?"

"Not a lot. I don't think he can."

"Like he's under a spell?"

"Maybe. I did see some flashing lights and a giant brown teddy bear with a yellow bow."

"The bear is weird."

"It's all weird," I told her. "Oh, and there was a levitating silver bow and arrow. It reminded me of a cupid's bow. What do you think it means?"

"Could be something. Could be nothing."

I made a face. "Now you're starting to sound like my dad."

She pressed her fingertips against her chest in mock indignation. "How dare you?"

I barked a laugh. "You're more fun than I thought you would be."

"Ditto," she said. "We should party sometime."

"If by party you mean drink wine and binge-watch fifteen seasons of *Supernatural*, then sure, let's party."

"Make it seven seasons of *Buffy The Vampire Slayer*, and it's a date."

I met her smile with my own. "It's a date."

A splash from the pool brought us back to reality. Carver pulled himself up onto the damp stone floor. He wrung his hair and wiped the water from his face.

"Well?" I asked anxiously.

"It's about fifteen meters. There are obstacles between here and where it opens up outside the cave. It took me a while to find the most direct route. But I can get you guys through it in less than a minute. I'll take you through it one at a time." He looked at the two of us and said, "It opens to a cove on the ocean."

"Yes!" Ryker pumped her fist. "When we get there, I have a spell key in my bag to get us into Natheria."

"Our bags," I said. "They're going to get soaked." My clothes could be washed, but I had my phone and my tablet to worry about.

"Mine are waterproof," Ryker said. "I have room for a few extra things, like your cell phone."

I cast her a grateful look. "Perfect. Thank you."

"Who goes first?" Carver asked.

"Take Ryker," I said. "That way, she can get ready to do whatever she needs to do to get us into Shangri-La."

"Are you sure?" Ryker's brow dipped. "You'll be alone."

I gave her a tight smile and held up my hand. "Go. I'm fine."

I gave Ryker my electronics, and she put them in one of her bags. Seconds later, she and Carver were gone, and I was alone.

I thought about the last time I'd seen Zev. The last time he'd held me in his arms, and not just in a dream. I'd wanted so badly to tell him how I'd never known love until I met him, but I'd been a coward. We'd only been intimate for a few short days, and telling him I was deeply, madly in love with him seemed like a rookie mistake.

I'd held back because I'd worried I would scare him off. *Silly bitch.* I rubbed my palms together, focused on Zev's symbol and closed my eyes. "Zev," I whispered. "I'm coming. Hold on."

"This is a surprise," a voice said. "Zev has a playmate. Or should I say...soulmate."

My eyes flew wide as I looked around the cavern. I was alone. Was the voice my imagination or something much more sinister? I grabbed my pack and my bag and waited by the water. The moment Carver surfaced, I took a deep breath trying to relax.

As I waded into the cool embrace of the pool, feeling its chill seep into my bones, I prepared myself for whatever Natheria had in store for me.

"You ready?" Carver asked.

"As ready as I'll ever be."

"Hold on to my waist," he said. "And don't let go."

I looped my fingers into his belt loop and let the water envelop me. As we plunged into the murky darkness, I couldn't get the disembodied voice from my mind. Each stroke propelled us forward through the murky depths, guided only by Carver's glowing body and the faint glimmer of light filtering from the cave entrance behind me.

The moment I thought my lungs would explode if I didn't exhale, we emerged from the depths. I gasped for air as the morning sun kissed my skin. A feeling of triumph and elation rushed through my veins. We'd done it. We'd escaped the cartel and the cave.

My victory was short-lived. Four men had Ryker on her knees in the sand, her hands behind her head. Three had their guns pointed at Carver and me. One had a gun pointed at Ryker's temple. That one said, "The two of you get out slowly and make your way over here."

The man had blond hair slicked back into a ponytail.

He wore a black combat outfit similar to the clothes my friend Luanne, an ex-mercenary, often wore. This didn't look or feel like a cartel.

"Who are you?" I asked. "And what do you want with us?"

"Look." He wagged the gun. "I'm just the delivery guy. I don't get paid to ask or answer questions."

Carver put himself between me and the merc. "Who sent you?"

"Someone who just wants to talk," the guy said.

"Who?" I pushed. "If it's just to talk, lower your weapons, answer the question, and we might cooperate."

"Fine." The man gestured to his cronies, who lowered their weapons. "We've been sent by the hunter."

I sucked in a breath at the unexpected answer. Zev's first message was about finding the hunter, and I'd done that. I crawled out of the water, looking like a fish thrown up on land. It was impossible to be graceful in wet cargo pants.

When I finally managed to stand, I held my head up with as much dignity as I could muster, which given my drowned rat status wasn't much, and said, "A deal's a deal. Take me to the hunter."

Chapter Ten

I MIGHT'VE BEEN HASTY IN AGREEING TO GO WITH four armed men to some undisclosed location without any concrete information, but from where I stood, we didn't have much choice. They had guns. We had our wit and charm. That and ten bucks might get us a cup of coffee, but it wouldn't overtake four combat-ready soldiers.

They put us in a large van—not the kind you saw in serial killer or heist movies, where the back was basically a psychopath's playground—thank heavens. This was a luxury van like you would see on a vacation tour. We had air conditioning, cushy seats, and large windows from which we could enjoy the view. All we needed were umbrella drinks and someone telling dad jokes to complete the vacation scenario.

Carver was allowed to put a shirt on before they stuck us in the middle seat. Ryker had given him one of hers, a Ramone's concert jersey circa 1972. Unfortunately, his boots had been left in the cave, and our "escorts" refused to let him go back for them. Two of the men settled into the row behind us, then a hulking bald mercenary got into the driver's seat, and the blond who'd done all the talking took the passenger side. Probably so he could have an unobstructed path to shoot us in the face if we tried anything funny. He didn't have to worry. We were not funny people—at least, I wasn't.

"What's your name?" I asked Blondie.

"Cooper," he said, keeping a wary eye on us. The man had an accent. It was slight enough that I hadn't noticed when he'd had a gun to Ryker's head. He pronounced Cooper like koo-pair and ended by barely skimming the r.

"Cooper, huh?" I scootched forward in my seat and angled my knees at him. "That's a strong name. Scottish, right?"

"Aye," he said, his gaze holding mine. "What's your name?"

"Mar—" Ryker nudged my knee, so I improvised. "Martina," I covered. "Martina King."

Martina made me think of Martina Navratilova, who made me think of Billie Jean King. The two rivals, who played fourteen championship matches against each other, were incredibly powerful athletes who equally advanced the notion of gender equality in sports. It seemed fitting to combine their names for my assumed moniker.

Cooper eyed me like he didn't believe me for one second. "Which one of you is Ryker?"

I bit my upper lip to keep from making a peep. Why had I thought the hunter was looking for me? And why was he or she or they looking for Ryker? And what did Zev have to do with all of this?

Before she could answer, Carver said, "That's me."

I was glad my lip was still between my teeth. What had possessed Carver to volunteer as tribute? The real Ryker couldn't either. "I'm Ryker," she said.

And because I watch too much television, I chirped in, "No, I'm Ryker."

"I thought you were Martina King."

"Yeah. Ryker Martina King," I said.

Cooper glared at the three of us for a moment, then began to laugh. "I could care less which one of you it is." He lowered his brow, and his glare became ten times more intimidating. "I get paid as long as Ryker is in the mix. The hunter can sort you out."

"Can you tell us about this hunter person?" I asked.

"I could." He grinned, and for the first time, I noticed that his teeth looked like they'd been filed to points. Like a shark's. "But I won't. Not unless you have money, you're willing to spend. I don't do anything for free."

"And what won't you do for money?"

"That's right." His grin grew more feral. "What won't I do for money." The other mercenaries laughed.

Oish. I leaned back in my seat, wishing I hadn't

asked. I made eye contact with Ryker, and she mouthed, "Not human."

Caught off guard, I flinched. I should've known they weren't human, considering the person who hired them ran a procurement business in the supernatural underbelly, but it still surprised me. "What are they?" I mouthed back.

"We are *na fir ghorma*." Cooper's response came with a smirk that betrayed his amusement.

"A what?" I asked, more confused than ever.

"A blue man," Carver remarked, shaking his head. "Otherwise known as a storm kelpie."

Cooper bared his teeth. "It's about time you recognized me, sylph. Your kind has always been too soft."

"And from what I know, your kind has always been a bunch of wave-stirring assholes," Carver shot back.

Oh no, I thought. Where was the practical, let's not get ourselves killed Carver of old? "Uhm, what he meant to say is..."

Carver's expression flattened. "I said what I said."

"It's a water-pissing contest," Ryker said under her breath. "Better to stay out of it."

"You want to know how we found you and your buddies?" Cooper leaned toward Carver. "I could smell you splashing around in the ocean from a mile away. What was that scent, lads?" He chuckled sinisterly and narrowed his gaze. "Chicken."

My friend blanched.

"And what's the best chicken?" I chimed in, because

I'm an idiot who can't stay out of it when a friend is getting bullied and sometimes doesn't have a brain-to-mouth filter. "It's chicken of the sea." I crossed my arms over my chest with a harumph.

"Agreed." Cooper turned his gaze on me and gnashed his gnarly teeth. "Mmmm, sea chicken is tasty."

My nose curled in revulsion. "Ew."

"Don't help," Ryker hissed. She stared at Cooper and his pals like they had grown four heads, and each one of them was spitting razor blades. "Let's try and survive the trip."

The fear I saw in her eyes chapped my ass. "Look," I said to Cooper. "Your job is to pick us up and drop us off. I think we can cut the chit-chat in the interim. As long as you have no idea which one of us is Ryker, then you can't kill us."

"Hunter didn't say Ryker had to be in one piece," he growled.

"I doubt that very much." My indignation was at an all-time high. What the hell was I doing? Not stopping, that's what. "I can't imagine the hunter wants Ryker..." I gestured between the three of us, "...injured. No one wants to pay for damaged goods, dick head. It's good business one-oh-one."

I heard an audible gasp at my audacity from one of the men in the back.

The tiny part of my brain that recognized when I was pushing the envelope echoed the sentiment, but there was no stopping me now. I was on a roll. "So, why don't you shove your idol threats, shut your yap-trap, and do your freaking job?"

You could hear a pin drop. The bald driver, his fingers white-knuckled on the wheel made a sharp turn and headed the van toward the ocean. My eyes widened as he hit the gas and we picked up speed.

"Wait? Is he driving us into the Pacific?"

Carver reached across Ryker and me as if to brace us for the impact. "You've got me," he said. "I've got you. Always."

The storm kelpies started laughing as the van filled with water. I was near the sliding door, but no matter how hard I yanked on it, it wouldn't budge. I shot a glance at Ryker and Carver. Carver looked as panicked as I did, but Ryker remained calmer than what was called for in this situation.

Quickly, I discovered why the storm kelpies were called blue men. When they submerged in the ocean, they all turned blue. Even their hair was blue, and they were covered in patterns that looked as if they'd been carved into their bodies. This was their real forms. Their mercenary appearance had been smoke and mirrors.

I relaxed when the water stopped at chest level and never rose any higher. We weren't sinking. I wasn't going to die. Those five words reduced my panic level from a ten to a five. I could face anything if I knew it wasn't going to kill me.

"Saltwater can hide and reveal," Ryker said. "Don't worry. We're safe. Ish," she added. "As safe as we can be with the bozos. They are taking us to Natheria." She pointed out to sea. I saw nothing but an enormous sandbar with little to no visible greenery. "It looks like a desert in the middle of the ocean."

"The fae are spectacular when it comes to illusion magic," she said. "But I've been here before. It's nothing like you've ever seen."

As we finished the ride to the island, I thought about how much I hated being in wet clothes. "I'm pretty sure this is a recipe for a rampant yeast infection," I uttered.

Ryker choked a laugh. "You really do just say whatever pops into your head."

I shrugged. "Not all the time, but it's harder to filter when I'm agitated."

"We're nearly there." She squeezed my hand. "This is going to be wild."

Wild was the understatement of the year.

One moment, we were up to our armpit in briny saltwater, the van eerily navigating the waves like a ghost ship, as the Isla de Altamura stretched out in front of us. Then, as if I'd dropped ten hits of acid and had shroom sauce for dessert, the van lurched forward, and we were draining sea water as the vehicle rolled into what could only be categorized as a dazzling display of excessive excess. My senses were overwhelmed as Big, Blue, and Bald parked on a street sandwiched between colorfully lit high-rise buildings crammed together so tightly that I couldn't see an alley between them. Each skyscraper seemed to vie for attention, adorned with a dizzying array of neon lights that danced and flickered in the night.

Wait. It was late morning when we passed through. "Did we skip some hours? Why is it nighttime already?"

"It's always night in Natheria," the bald driver said.

"Awesome." I blinked at the sea of technicolor chaos. Natheria looked like Vegas of the future on steroids had given birth to a baby that also took steroids.

Neon signs flashed and blinked, advertising every-thing from unusual cuisine to exotic drugs, and forbidden pleasures.

Cooper opened the door and the rest of the water dumped out of the van and onto the ground. "Get out," he ordered.

It was like stepping into another world. The air crackled with energy and magic coursing through the streets like an electric current. But the glitz and glam couldn't cover the stench of decay in the air.

"There's nothing like Natheria," Ryker murmured, her voice barely audible over the city's din. And she was right—at least it was like nothing that I'd ever seen. Natheria was a place of contradictions, where beauty and depravity walked hand in hand.

"This place is impossible." Something large roared above me, and I jerked to duck away with the cat-like reflexes of someone who hits her head on stuff a lot. "Was that a flying motorcycle?"

"Probably," Ryker said. "Anything you can imagine, Natheria has it."

If that were the case, I'd imagine Zev safe and away from this awful place. Which meant getting this shit show on the road. I glowered at Cooper, who was now over six feet tall. WTF? "Well, big guy," I said. "Take us to your leader."

Chapter Eleven

COOPER LED THE WAY WITH HIS MEN FLANKING US AS we entered a vivid carmine red door on a nearby building. We traversed a corridor that seemed too long for the building we entered. Was this like a Doctor Who situation? Was the inside of the building even bigger than the outside? Torches in silver sconces were set along the black-painted walls, and the shadows they cast looked like a mass of writhing bodies engaged in very orgy-like behavior. Eeep.

"Is that...?" Carver asked.

"Yep," I responded. "I think it is."

"How do they get the shadows to so accurately depict..." He pursed his lips and gave a quick head shake. "You know what, I don't want to know."

There was something shiny floating above another carmine door.

Ryker nudged me. "It's a cupid's bow and arrow," she whispered.

I blinked as the floating object came into focus. Holy crap. It was a silver bow and arrow like the one that I'd seen in my last Zev dream. "What do you think it means?"

"No clue." She handed me a strip she'd torn from her t-shirt. "For your hand."

I took the damp fabric and wrapped my left hand until my palm was completely covered. "Thank you." I'd been warned to hide my hand from Zev, Carver, and Ryker, and I would think, yeah, no brainer. Duh. Then something would happen, like being held at gunpoint, and I would forget. I couldn't keep doing that. I reminded myself on repeat, *hide the symbol like your life depends on it.* Because I believed my life did depend on it. And maybe Zev's did, too.

How long did it take to walk down one freaking hallway? "Are we almost there?" I asked Cooper.

"We'll get there when we get there," he said. "Sometimes it takes seconds, sometimes minutes."

Baldy added, "I walked this hall for an hour the first time I was summoned."

Cooper grunted. "The hunter likes to study his visitors before he admits them into his office."

"Study?" I scanned the hall for a camera. It was too dark in the recesses of the hallway to see any, but the most disturbing thing I found was that the door we'd walked in minutes earlier was only about ten feet behind us. "What the hell is this place?" I reached back and grabbed Ryker's hand. "I don't feel good about this."

"Is this the first time you're not feeling good about this?" She squeezed my hand. "Because this has been pretty fucked since the beach."

It seriously was. But I hadn't felt the weight of our situation until now. I'd been so wrapped up in finding Zev that I hadn't stopped to wonder why the hunter had hired the goons to bring Ryker in.

This probably should've been a question for earlier, but my brain didn't always work linearly. I'd always been very good at compartmentalizing. This is why, up until now, I hadn't been freaking out about the fact that a part of Zev was inside of me and not the fun part.

Or that I'd picked a fight with a seven-foot-tall blue guy who could use water to sink entire ships while we were surrounded by water. Not to mention that I hitched a ride on an uncharted plane to travel to a magical city to rescue an ifrit who may or may not even want my help.

On top of that, I'd coerced the sweetest, nicest eclectic witch person I'd ever met into joining me on this suicide mission.

Honestly, out of everything racing through my brain, the catastrophic spell that bound Zev's soul to me, the spontaneous combustion, the emergency landing, getting chased by the cartel, and being captured by four storm kelpies, putting Carver in danger was the thing that made me feel the worst.

I reached for Carver. He took my bandaged hand in

his. "I'm sorry," I said. "You wouldn't be in this mess if it weren't for me."

"You knew I wasn't going to let you do this on your own," he said. "No need for sorrys. We're in this together."

"The three amigos," Cooper snarked. "You do realize we can all hear your bleeding hearts."

"Better than smelling your butt," I retorted.

The blue guy laughed. "I don't hate you, feeble woman. You have the fire of a kelpie, even if your fragile body would split apart at the first mating."

"The feeling is not mutual," I spat. "And I'd stomp your dick so hard it would be the only thing splitting. Misogynistic cryptozoid."

All the stupid kelpies started laughing again.

"I'm glad I can amuse you."

"As am I, *Martina*. As am I," Cooper said.

"That's Ryker to you," I said, feeling salty.

Ugh. These blue men had pushed all the wrong buttons, and I was getting sick and tired of games. Suddenly, the shadow orgy turned into a murder spree, and every writhing figure on the walls was stabbing and punching each other.

"I've had enough of this." I let go of Carver's hand and started reaching for torches. I grabbed the first one and threw it down on the floor. Then the next and the next.

"What are you doing?" Baldy asked.

"I'm making my own path," I told him.

Ryker let out a quiet, "hell yeah!" Then she started grabbing torches as well. The blue men tried to stop us, but my anger made me quick on my feet. Carver grabbed a torch as well, and the guy behind Baldy smacked him in the head, smashing his face into the wall. Carver's nose began to bleed.

"Hey!" I flung the torch I held at him, and the arrow prongs at the top lodged into his chest. My eyes flew wide as he yanked it out and scowled as if he was going to murder me. "Uhm. My bad."

Baldy put out an arm to stop his buddy from charging me. "We will kill them when they no longer serve a purpose for the hunter."

The bloody-chested blue man barked like a seal.

"Yes," Baldy told him. "We can eat her first." He grinned at me when he said it, the sadistic jerk.

The hunter's door rapidly appeared just a few feet away. "Hah," I said triumphantly. "Got your attention, didn't I?"

Cooper, seriously annoyed with me now—mission accomplished—flung the door open and shoved me inside an empty white room. Carver and Ryker were tossed in as well, and when they hit my back, we crumpled to the ground in a dog pile.

"Cretins," a young man cried out. "We don't treat guests like rubbish in my establishment." He had long, curly brown hair that brushed his hips, sharp facial features like they drew in Manga comics, and a lot of freckles across his pert nose. He didn't look any older than Michael, so his white button-down shirt open to his naval made me uncomfortable. He popped a fan and waved it at the storm kelpies. "Shoo flies," he ordered. "Don't bother me."

The fact that all the blue men quickly backed away without hesitation told me this young man was more substantial and powerful than he looked. His tight leather hipster jeans flared at the bottom, and he wore black patent leather platform boots that caught odd winks of light as he paced the floor.

"I'm so sorry, my friends," he said. His voice was smooth, not high-pitched, but still had the resonance of youth. "This isn't how I wanted to meet you."

"Why did you want to meet us?" I asked as we all scrambled to our feet.

"Not us," he stated. "The infamous Ryker. Always in the shadows. Always gets his—" he looked at Carver "—or her—" he moved his gaze to Ryker than me, "—man." He casually waved his fingers in a flourish. "Or creature or whatever. I am a talented procurer, but I think you could give me a run for my money. When I found out you had searched for me on the subworld message boards, I couldn't let the opportunity to meet you pass me by."

Was this about a business rivalry? Had the hunter brought us here to size up the competition? I didn't think so. Someone in this guy's position wouldn't be frivolous with his actions—not unless they suited some higher purpose.

"Eanie meanie miney moe, which one of you is Ryker?"

"Can't you tell?" I couldn't keep the sarcasm from my voice. I blamed wet panties and low blood sugar. "You are the hunter, after all."

He pinned me with a curious stare. "I am at that." He walked a circle around me. "You are a curious one," he said. "What are you?" Tapping his chin, he studied me much in the same way Ryker had when we first met. "Giant, yes. Some learned witchcraft. But there is something else..."

I clenched my bandaged fist. "Nope, that's it. Human, giant, witch. You nailed me."

"Oh, not yet, I haven't, but I'd be delighted."

"Yuck. You're young enough to be my nephew."

"My dear child." He put a finger under my chin and tilted my head back. "I am as old as time itself."

A bark of amusement escaped me. "Then you should be a lot better at this." *Holy crap, Marigold. Shut the hell up!*

The hunter looked shocked for a moment, but he began to laugh instead of lashing out at me. "You are quite abrasive. I find it charming."

It seemed the more you hated a man, the more he wanted you. Ugh. "Get some self-esteem. It would serve you well."

Carver's eyes bugged. I didn't know whether he was upset with me or trying not to laugh. Ryker, however, looked nervous and scared. Uh oh. She was the one who could read auras. Maybe caution was warranted.

Thankfully, the hunter wasn't fazed by my witty rapport. "Tell me, Ryker," he addressed the three of us. "Why were you searching for me?"

"We're looking for someone who might've been a client of yours. Someone important to me." I met the hunter's gaze. "An ifrit named Za'fir."

A slow smile spread across the hunter's face, and his eyes alighted with humor. "You know Zev?" He placed his hand on my shoulder. "We are old friends, he and I. Why didn't you say so sooner?" He wiped the air with his hands as if swiping right on a dating app, and the entire room instantly transformed. The air was heavy with the aroma of crisp exotic spices like cardamom, anise, and cinnamon. A pattern of mosaic tiles lined the walls, depicting scenes better left to the imagination. This guy might be old as dirt, but he had the taste of a pubescent teenager.

A wall fountain trickled gently, adding to the ambiance. Plush cushions with gold brocaded seams were on the floor in front of a round, ornately carved tea table, complete with a teapot and cups in the center. "Please, come sit. We'll have tea, and you can tell me what kind of trouble my dear Za'fir has gotten himself into."

I glanced at my companions. Neither of them gave me the signal to run.

"Okay," I agreed. "Let's have some tea and chat."

Chapter Twelve

I SMELLED THE TEA, BUT I DIDN'T DRINK IT. I'D watched too many true crime documentaries with my oldest sister, Dahlia, and it felt unsafe to take an open drink from a stranger.

"You don't like tea?" the hunter asked with a smile that didn't reach his eyes.

"I love tea." I gave him a thin smile in return but didn't reach for my cup. "So, let's talk about Zev. You say you're old friends." In the dream, Zev had told me to find the hunter. Maybe this guy was telling the truth about his relationship with the ifrit. Still, there was something about the hunter that felt seedy to me. Maybe it was the sex and violence of the pictographs, and maybe it was just a gut feeling. "But first, do you go by Hunter or the hunter?"

I was surprised and kind of shocked that Ryker and

Carver were happy to let me take the lead. I felt like I was constantly putting my foot in my mouth, but so far, it hadn't gotten us killed. That was a win in my book.

The hunter's eyes softened. "My friends call me Shay."

Ryker did a spit-take, then began to cough.

Carver patted her back. "Are you okay?"

"Yeeep," she rasped. "Fine." She'd obviously had suspicions about the hunter, and his name had seemed to confirm it for her.

Whatever Ryker knew, it would have to wait. The matter at hand was pressing. "Did Zev come to see you in the past seven months?" I pivoted my knees toward the man, and my wet cargo pants made a weird farty noise. "My pants got wet in the ocean."

"Sure," Shay said, arching his brow. "That sounds reasonable." There was a playful glint in his eyes. "As to your question, yes, Zev came to see me in the past year. He wanted me to find someone for him."

"Who?"

"A hexogenist."

I frowned. "What's that?" Iris's gnome called sorcerers *hexenmeisters*. Hex was a spell—well, a curse. And genist ... I wasn't sure. "Is it some kind of witch?" The "o" might make the creature masculine. Or a warlock, or a male witch or sorcerer?" I was doing mental gymnastics, and Shay was giving me nothing. "Well? What's a hexogenist?"

"Ah," he said in a clipped tone. "I thought you had it for a moment. A hexogenist is a sorcerer who specializes in gene morphing."

"Why in the world would Zev want to find a—" I stopped short as the why hit me in the face. "He wanted someone to take his fire." My voice sounded hollow to my ears.

"Oh, yuck," Shay said. "Why would he want that? Zev's fire is the best thing about him."

This guy had never slept with Zev because if he had, he would've known there were some other pretty darn good things about my missing djinn. "Who knows, Shay? People are strange."

"Well, well. You have called me by my name. This makes us friends." He peered at me over his teacup as he took a noisy sip. After he asked, "What may I call you?"

"Anytime you want, as long as it's not late for supper," I said, quoting one of my dad's favorite sayings. "Did you find a hexogenist?"

Shay produced a toothpick and began to chew on the end. "I did," he admitted. "A sorcerer by the name of Maxim Raine out of Switzerland. He is a renowned geneticist who also dabbles in magic. His field of research combines both crafts to manipulate DNA at the source."

"Seriously? That sounds like some Frankenstein shit," Ryker said, piping up for the first time.

"Oh, little djinn. You have finally come out to play." Shay wiggled his freckled nose at her as if she were a cute puppy. I half expected him to follow up with a boop. I was grateful when it didn't happen. "It is, as you so eloquently put, some Frankenstein shit. His early experiments were a horror factory of mistakes." He flicked the toothpick behind him, and I watched it disappear midair. "But his work has gotten much better over the past two decades."

"Twenty years?" Disgust was written on Carver's face. "That's criminal."

"One man's crime is another's salvation, my friend," Shay said. He was getting real casual throwing that word around. "Dr. Raine has saved many lives with his research and magic. But his clinic is a well-kept secret, and he doesn't disclose his use of magic to his clients. They think his work is all science."

Rowan's words came back to me. *Magic is just science that hasn't been discovered yet.* "Did he go to see this Raine guy?"

"As far as I know," Shay told us with a shrug. "I haven't seen him since I sent him on his way."

I struggled against the overwhelming disappointment that washed over me upon discovering Zev was no longer in Natheria. We'd barely been away for two days, but it had felt like we'd been on this journey for a month already. I was sure we'd finally catch up with Zev in this place, but finding the hunter had just been the beginning of the quest.

There were so many challenges to overcome. Ryker's

plane needed parts, and it was probably surrounded by a small army. Even if we did have the stuff to fix her aircraft and the cartel had given up and gone home, we had no transportation to get back to the mainland. How in the world were we supposed to get out of Natheria, let alone get to Switzerland? I am not dying, I told myself, but it didn't feel as reassuring as it usually did, considering we'd—well, I—had made enemies of four grumpy and seriously dangerous blue dudes who wanted to eat us for dinner, but definitely not in a fun way.

"Shay," I said sweetly. "I don't suppose you know of a quick way to get back to Sinaloa?"

He smiled. "I could help you," he replied. "For a price, of course."

I lived on a teacher's salary, which left me out. I looked to Ryker and Carver.

"The payment doesn't have to be money," Shay pointed out. "I will give you safe passage from my island if you show me what's under the bandage on your hand."

I tucked my arm behind my back. "I'm good," I said.

Carver started muttering, but I couldn't hear what he was saying. As Shay got up and took a step toward me, Ryker sprung to her feet.

"I'll pay," she said quickly. "I have bitcoin I could transfer immediately. Cash. That would take a bit longer. Same for gold. Gemstones? I can get my hands on those as well. What's your price?"

Holy crap. Ryker was "name your price" rich.

"No," Shay brushed his flowing locks behind his shoulders. "I want my first price."

Carver stopped muttering and shouted, "Sanctum." A circle appeared around us, glowing with energy. The eclectic witch had set a protection spell while Shay was distracted by Ryker and me.

"Nice." I nodded my approval and then turned to the hunter. "My answer is no. You don't get to see my hand."

Shay's brows furrowed in anger; his rage barely contained. Right when I thought he was about to explode, he started laughing—it was a down to the belly, tears leaking from the eyes, total guffaw. He threw his hands around the room, shifting and shaking, ever-changing until we were back in an empty white room. The hunter snapped his fingers, and a cage dropped around the three of us.

"I can wait," he said.

"For what?" I asked.

"For you to get so dehydrated and hungry that you beg me to free you. You will show me your hand and let me examine your palm, or I'll wait until you are dead, and I will do it without your permission. I'm a patient man."

I didn't think that last statement was true. I glanced at my friends. "Any ideas?"

They both shook their heads.

Well, damn. "I don't think it leaves us much choice then. I have to let him check out my hand."

Ryker grabbed my wrist. "He is Shay," she stated as if I wasn't already aware of the hunter's name.

"I know."

"No." She grew more emphatic. "He is Shay. He's a determiner. The Egyptians sometimes worshiped him as the god of fate."

"What does that mean for us?" I asked.

"That I already know your futures." Shay smirked. "I see all."

I didn't buy it. Shay was an all-powerful god, but he was trying to bargain with us. It made no sense. There was something fishy about Shay, and it wasn't that his home was on the ocean.

"Uh-uh," I said, addressing Ryker and Carver. "The gods are not gods, and no one is truly immortal. My sister killed a fire god, and he'd been around since before the dinosaurs." I spun around to face Shay. I pointed an accusing finger at him. "And if that guy could tell the future, he would've seen Carver throw the protection circle."

Wait, wait. My thoughts raced to the beginning of our time with the hunter. He had pressed a finger under my chin. Wouldn't he have been able to see my fate if it was merely touching? No. I thought. It has to be more than that. There's a loophole to all bargains, Zev had told me once. You only need to find it. What was Shay's loophole?

I snapped my fingers. The answer hit me quick. I crossed my fingers and hoped I was correct. "You asked permission to examine my hand. You need consent in order to access your gift of foretelling. Otherwise, why ask when you have all this power to take what you want?"

"Oooo," Shay crooned. "You are such a clever one." He shrugged. "You got me. However, it doesn't change the fact that you're trapped in a prison, and I can keep you in there until your eyeballs dry from your sockets and fall out of your head."

"Evocative." I gave him a grim smile. "But no deal." I tested the metal bars of our cage. "You said something about salt water and illusion spells," I directed to Ryker. "Is this an illusion? Or is this prison real?"

"It's hard to tell, but I think it's an illusion. Making actual matter appear and disappear the way he does would expend a tremendous amount of energy."

I arched my brow at her. "Does he look tired to you?"

"Nope," she replied.

"Stop talking," Shay snapped.

"Make me," I spat back. "Carver, our clothes are still wet with the ocean. Can you use that to create a spell to break the illusion?"

"I definitely can."

"Awesome." I took off my baggy sweater and handed it to him. The yarn was still dripping. "Let's get the hell out of here."

"You can't do this," Shay seethed. "I won't let you leave."

I locked eyes with him. "In the immortal words of Dean Winchester, shut your cakehole."

"I tried to be nice, but no more." Shay stalked to the cage, reached in, and snatched me by the throat. "Protection circles don't work on gods."

"Good...to...know," I croaked. My palm itched as Shay yanked me through the cage, the bars passing through my body as if I were a ghost.

"Show me your hand." He shook me like a forty-seven-year-old rag doll. I was pretty sure he'd knocked some of my parts loose.

The itching grew intense as the pressure on my neck made it hard to breathe. I smelled the smoke before I saw it and knew exactly what was happening. If he wanted to see, he was going to get more than he bargained for.

I slammed my palm against Shay's freckled face, and my hand burst into flames. He screamed as his skin melted under my touch, then threw me down when his hair caught on fire. The cage disappeared. The white room turned back into the tearoom—which meant the white room was the illusion—and Shay's face was no longer manga cutesy with a smattering of trendy freckles. Instead, he had beady eyes, big round cheeks, and a snout that resembled a pig. He stuck his face into the wall fountain to negate the effects of my flames. I shook my hand, but the fire took a second to subside.

"Let's go," Carver shouted. "Run!"

And on that excellent suggestion, we exited the carmine door and found ourselves back on the street. "Where, too?" I asked.

"This way." Ryker pointed to the right. "I know a guy."

There wasn't time for questions. Shay would be after us soon, or he'd send his goons. Either way, we had to be somewhere else and fast. Ryker's "guy" was as good a place to run as anywhere else. Hopefully, he could help us find a way out of Natheria that didn't end with us roasting on a storm kelpie's spit.

Chapter Thirteen

We ran for what felt like a mile before cutting through an arch that had been braced between two buildings. It opened to another street with more cramped high-rises. We were on the run for at least twenty minutes when Ryker finally stopped in front of a door with an awning that said, "Francois's Fix It Shop." There was a sign that said, *you break it, I buy it* in the window.

Ryker rang the doorbell before pounding on the door.

"What is it?" a man's gruff voice answered. "It's the middle of the night."

"Isn't it always the middle of the night here?" I asked Ryker.

"Yes," she replied. "Martel, it's me. Open up."

The door swung in, and a large man, built like Superman, with pearlescent hair and a heavy beard, stood in the frame. "Neetra, my love."

Neetra? I gave Carver an askance look.

He gave me an "I don't know" head shake.

Martel's face was lit up with joy as he stared at the half-djinn. "It's been too long since you last returned."

"It has," she agreed. "I need your help." She gestured to Carver and me. "*We* do. I need a way to the mainland that flies under the hunter's radar. We got some storm kelpies hot on our asses as well."

"I can make the arrangements." He grabbed her into his arms, and when his hair dropped back, I saw he had long, pointy Spock ears. "But first, we make love."

Ryker grinned. "You read my mind." She wrapped her legs around his waist as he carried her inside.

Carver and I stood on the stoop as Martel carried our friend through the door. Unsure what to do, but knowing that standing in the street made us sitting ducks for blue dudes, I spoke. "I suppose we go in... No invitation needed, I guess."

Carver nodded. "Yep. Doesn't seem like."

As we entered the dimly lit shop, the old floorboards creaking beneath us, the air was thick with the scent of oil, lemons, and aged wood. Shelves lined the walls with all kinds of strange items and a few mundane items, like clocks and radios. There didn't seem to be any rhyme or reason for where the items ended up. A glowing Crystal orb was sandwiched between an old manual typewriter and a blender.

Ryker let out a squeal of delight as her "guy" threw her over his shoulder and carried her caveman-style up the stairs. She waved at us, a smile on her lips. "Make yourself comfortable while we hammer out a few details."

I had a good idea of what was fixing to get hammered out. The situation was beyond absurd, but I just gave her a knowing smile and waved back. "Have fun."

Carver closed the door behind us. Beaded sweat dotted his forehead, and his pale skin was flushed pink. He limped across the floor, and I noticed his socked feet had taken a battering. Bright red blood soaked the fabric near his left big toe.

"You're bleeding."

"Better than the alternative." He heel walked his way over to a couch in what appeared to be a waiting area and peeled off his sock. His toenail had partially detached, and it looked seriously painful.

"Ow. When did you do that?" In the corner of the area, there was a water cooler with a small table next to it that held a one-cup coffeemaker, napkins, and stacked foam cups. I got Carver a cup of water and some napkins to clean his wound.

"It's cold," I said, holding it out.

He smiled as he took the cup. "Want to see something neat?"

"Always." I sat on the worn leather couch next to him as he set the cup on the ground and dipped his mangled toe into the water. He gave it a swirl, the water going from clear to pink and back to clear. When he took his toe out, it was completely healed. "Ta-dah," he said softly.

"Amazing." I quietly applauded and mimed an audience's cheers. "The crowd goes wild." I took the cup and set it down on the end table at my right. "You're getting good with the water stuff."

"I've been trying to practice as much as I can. A lot of it is built-in instinct, but some things, like healing myself with water, takes more effort." Carver's proximity to my sister when she had triggered her nero-craft had ignited his dormant sylph half. Since then, he'd been trying to learn the way of his mother's people. Had Cooper Sharkbutt's words struck a nerve or released insecurity? Carver had acted out of character by trading jibes with the storm kelpie, and I worried there was more going on.

"You're doing great," I reassured him. "And you're not soft. You are so brave. I'm sorry I got you into this mess, but I'm glad you're with me." I snickered as I thought about his argument with the blue man. "I said what I said, huh?"

He looked mildly abashed. "That guy gave me the full ragey."

"Ya think?"

Carver gave me an assessing look. "Are you okay? What's going on with you?"

"Whatever could you mean?" I fake-tossed my hair for dramatic effect. "I am super-duper."

"Hah." He rolled his eyes. "You have such a quick and agile mind. I always see it when you're learning new spells or crafting your own. You catch on fast, and you can see how new ingredients have the potential to change the outcomes. It's incredible. I can see you becoming a great creator one day, with witches from all over eager to learn your recipes."

"I feel a *but* coming on," I teased.

"But," he said, confirming my suspicion. "You take so many unnecessary risks. You put yourself in danger without thinking about the consequences. I swear I've aged twenty years since you modified the guidance potion. Nineteen of those years have been just since we got on the plane."

"I'm sorry. I'd like to tell you that I'll do better and take fewer risks, but I'd be lying. I mean, I'll try." I gave an 'eh' gesture. "I don't like being in these situations any more than you do, but I can't help but act when they happen. I'm a doer, damn it, and doers are going to do."

He chuckled. "You should put that on a t-shirt and sell it."

I patted his leg. "Would you like a hug?"

"Yes, please."

I wrapped my arms around Carver and held on until he'd had enough. Truthfully, I needed the hug as much as he did—maybe more.

"More water, I think. And not for your toe. If we have more running to do, staying hydrated is key."

"Please, dear Goddess, no more running," Carver lamented. "Running is the worst."

"Amen," I chuckled as I went to the water cooler and poured us a couple of cups.

We swiftly gulped down our first cups of water and

went back for more. I was sure we were suffering from mild dehydration and low blood sugar.

As Carver and I lounged in the cozy yet cluttered confines of the fix-it shop, it sunk in that Zev wasn't in Natheria. We'd come all this way, and he hadn't been here for months. The trail was cold at this point. Even so, I would track down Dr. Raines and force him to tell me what he did with the ifrit. The way Shay had spoken about the mad magical scientist, I worried that Zev might've become another "mistake" in his experiments, and he was trapped in some vat of slime deep in the basement of an illegal research facility, growing extra arms, four noses, and a foot out his ass.

I dismissed the thought as soon as it entered my head. I wouldn't doom-scroll all the scenarios. I was going to find him, and then I would know. Until that time, I had to keep hope and faith in my guy that he was the cunning djinn who tricked a thousand-year-old sultan out of immortality. He would keep himself safe or at least unharmed.

"I wish we still had those protein bars," Carver remarked, sinking deeper into the couch's worn leather cushions.

His words brought me back to the present. "What?"

"I'm starving," he said, a hint of longing in his voice.

"I wish I had dry underwear," I retorted with a smirk, my gaze wandering around the cluttered space.

Carver chuckled at my response, a sound that

mingled with the soft hum of machinery in the background. "Sure, that too."

My stomach rumbled again, a reminder of its empty state. "A protein bar sounds good, too," I admitted, absently rubbing my belly. "We expended a lot of energy today."

Leaning forward, I rested my elbows on my knees, the damp fabric of my cargo pants rough against my skin. "Is it even still today?" I mused, a hint of fatigue tingeing my words. "It feels like we've been gone for a month."

Carver's eyes scanned the room as if searching for answers amidst the clutter. "I think so, but it's hard to tell," he replied, his voice thoughtful. "I don't trust anything when it comes to this place." His stomach made a sharp, trill sound. He made a face. "Maybe we should go on a snack hunt?"

"I'm in," I agreed, rising from the couch to join him in our quest for sustenance. As we moved through the shop, my mind drifted to Ryker's enigmatic friend, Martel.

"What do you think of Ryker's fella?" I asked curiously. "When she said she knew a guy, I hadn't seen him coming, did you? He and Ryker seem, uhm, very close."

Carver tilted his head in a half-shrug. "She's part of that free love generation," he remarked casually, his gaze flitting across the shelves and workbenches. "A love the one you're with kind of attitude."

"He is hot," I admitted, a hint of admiration in my voice. "If you like that sort of type."

Carver nodded in agreement, his lips quirking into a

faint smile. "Who doesn't like that type?" he smirked. "Pretty easy on the eyes."

I giggled, a lightness creeping into my mood despite the lingering hunger. "Dude," I exclaimed, giving him a playful whack on the arm. "Did you see those ears? Do you think he's an elf?"

"I've never met an elf, so I'm not sure," he admitted, a note of amusement in his voice. "But I have so many questions."

"Oh my gosh, me too." I looped my elbow in his. "Let's find food and discuss."

"Deal."

As we combed the shadowy corners of the fix-it shop, the search for snacks took on a life of its own, a welcome distraction from the danger we faced. When one of the doors opened to a small kitchen, complete with a microwave and stove, I shouted, "Bingo, baby!"

I opened the refrigerator. "There's a hard yellow cheese, some kind of smoked meat log, and grapes," I informed Carver.

He rifled through the cabinets. "I've got soda crackers, jam of some kind, and," he opened a drawer below the counter, "a knife." He held up the shiny blade in triumph. "This feast is on," he said.

"Like Donkey Kong," I agreed.

Twenty minutes later, as we were relaxed, I regretted the last piece of cheese I had eaten. "Too much," I said. "Way too much."

"Same," Carver lamented. "I have a meat and cheese baby growing in my tummy."

Ryker came down the stairs with some extra pep in her step, holding something in her arms. Her hair was damp, and she wore clean, dry clothes, which I thought was cheating. "Martel has a way out for us, but it will take a few hours to arrange. He had some extra sweats he offered for you both. You can use his bathroom to clean up, but make your shower quick. His hot water heater isn't big, and warm water runs out fast.

"Dibs," I said quickly. I was getting a raw patch on my inner thigh because of my damp pants, and I was desperate to get into something warm and dry.

"There's a washer and dryer in a laundry room near the bathroom if you want to wash and dry your stuff while we wait to leave," Ryker informed us. "There's time. We should all get a nap in, too. Once we get moving, I'm not sure when we will be able to rest." She scratched her cheek as she looked at the tray of mostly eaten sliced cheese and smoked sausage. "I hope you saved some of that for me. I'm famished."

I grinned. "I bet you are."

She pursed her lips and threw the sweats at me. "Sometimes, when you get an itch, you have to scratch it."

Martel came down the stairs and said, "And nobody scratches an itch like Neetra." He gave Ryker a fond smile. "My contact will meet you all in the Brownie District."

I frowned. "Because it's brown?"

"No," Martel said. "Because it's run by Brownies, and they are the only ones on this island that aren't afraid of the hunter. His magic doesn't work on them, and no amount of money will convince a kelpie to step foot in their territory. Brownies don't play nice or fair." He eyeballed the food. "I see you helped yourself. Good. My pop always said that a full guest is a tasty guest." He cracked a wry smile. "Just kidding. Not about pop saying it, but—" he rolled his hand to emphasize. "I don't eat people anymore."

My eyes widened. "Anymore?"

"He's a reformed orc," Ryker said. "Now, he only eats wild game and fish meat. Anything that walks on two legs is safe."

"I'll let the animals around here know." I wasn't joking. Yeesh. But hey, the question was answered. Martel was an orc. Who knew they could be handsome?

"Why does everyone around here eat people?" Carver asked. "Cripes."

"Evolutionary food chain, my friend," Martel said. "Humans are somewhere in the middle."

"This has been fun," I said, doing my best to hide my wince. "But I'd be grateful if you would direct me to your bathroom."

Martel pointed at the stairs. "Up four flights of steps and to the left. Second door on the right."

"Four flights?" That seemed like a long way to walk if your bladder was full.

"That's my guest bathroom," he explained, as if

reading my thoughts. "There's a bedroom on that floor as well if you want to rest when you're finished."

I gave him a grateful nod. "Thank you, Martel, for your food, hospitality, and getting us out of Natheria."

"I haven't gotten you out yet, but you're welcome."

Once I reached the shower, my tweaked knee from running through the forest was re-tweaked. Ugh. Even so, I wasted no time stripping off the wet, uncomfortable clothes. The orc's shampoo, conditioner, and body wash all smelled woodsy with sweet notes of vanilla.

The bedroom had a window with a bench. I dressed, leaned against the ledge, and looked out onto the bustling city. I was high enough to get a full view of the city lights, which, from a distance, reminded me of Christmas. There were lights on the front of the buildings. A different color for each one—blue, yellow, green, yellow, yellow, blue, and red. My mouth went dry as I went through the colors again. *Blue, yellow, green, yellow, yellow, blue, and red.*

I hopped up and sprinted out of the guest room and into the hallway. I collided with Carver as he was coming out of the bathroom.

"What's wrong?" he asked, his expression worried. "You look like you've seen a ghost."

I grabbed his arms to steady myself. "Zev might still be in Natheria," I told him. "We have to go. There is a giant teddy bear with the yellow bow out there some-where, and I'm going to find it."

"I don't get it." He narrowed his gaze on me. "Are you sure you're okay?"

"I'll explain when we get downstairs." Gripping his hand, I dragged him toward the stairs. "I saw the flashing colors. I have to tell Ryker, and if we only have a few hours before our escape from this island leaves, we have to go now."

First, I'd seen the cupid's bow from my dream at the hunter's place, and now the colorful flashing lights. It had to mean something, even if it was a coincidence. Regardless, I couldn't leave this place until I knew for certain.

Chapter Fourteen

"The dream," I explained to the group, "had three elements. The silver cupid's bow, the flashing lights, and the giant teddy bear with a big yellow bow. I've seen the bow and the lights, and I have this gut feeling that if we find the bear, I'll find Zev."

I was grateful and a little surprised my companions didn't look at me like I was crazy.

"Do you think the hunter lied?" Carver asked. "About the hexogenist," he added for clarity. "That seems oddly specific and elaborate."

Martel, who remained silent for the whole explanation about Zev and my dreams, said, "The hunter is a high lord of the fae-folk. He can bend and stretch the truth, but he can't tell an outright lie. If he says your ifrit came seeking a hexogenist, he probably did."

"I thought Shay was an Egyptian god," I said.

Martel laughed. "Many fae high lords were idolized

as divine beings. Their formidable magical talents are eclipsed only by their vanity and arrogance. They think they're untouchable, but their ego is their weakness."

"Check. Shay is fae, not god." I hadn't believed he was a god, but it was good to have confirmation. "He's still a problem. I'm sure his blue baboons are scouring the city for us."

"And more," Martel agreed. "Shay may be a spoiled brat, but he is also the most powerful creature in Natheria. No one will cross him, apart from the Brownies. He doesn't worry about them because they aren't strong enough to take over the city. Like I said before, fae high lords have huge egos. He's wrong to ignore them, but he lets them do as they will, and they stay out of his territories."

We'd gotten off-topic, but I was glad to learn more about Shay. Know your enemy and all that.

"So, if he can't lie, then he did find a hexogenist for Zev," Carver said. "He also said Zev left the island six months ago. Do we assume that's the truth?"

I shook my head in emphatic denial. "He didn't say Zev left Natheria. He said that he hadn't seen Zev since he sent him on his way. He didn't specify where he sent him, either. Just that he sent him." My palm started to prickle as my anger escalated into fury. "Zev is still on Natheria. I can feel it in my bones."

"Your bones are smoking," Ryker said. "Please don't set Martel's store on fire. I like him, and I like his place."

"Aw, babes," Martel cooed. "I like you too."

Ryker flashed a pleased smile but then got right back to business. "Get your fire under control."

I shook my hand out and flexed my fingers. After a few deep breaths, the smoking stopped. "I don't know how to control it," I said. "Good for the people of Natheria because if I could, I would burn this whole place down to find Zev." I closed my eyes, fighting back frustrated tears. "I don't mean it, Martel. I'm just so angry right now." I opened my eyes. "And scared. Not just for me but for us, and mostly for Zev, because I feel like he's in serious trouble."

Carver pulled me into a sideways hug, his arm a reassuring weight around my shoulders. "Your feelings are valid," he assured me, his voice steady and comforting.

"Thank you." Sometimes, having all these strings of thoughts and constant connections running through my mind made me feel nuts. It was nice to be validated. "I appreciate you saying so."

"Feelings are great," Ryker observed, her voice soft amidst the tension. "But they aren't going to get us downtown unseen. Shay will have eyes everywhere."

Carver glanced at the orc, contemplating. "Maybe Martel can show us a backway to get there. With a local guide, we might make it unseen."

"Could you?" I turned to Martel, hoping for a positive response.

"Sorry, no can do," Martel replied briskly, shaking his head. He gave Ryker a sympathetic look. "I love this little package of dynamite." His tone shifted to serious. "But I still gotta live here. If the hunter finds out I'm helping you, that will be the end for me and my business."

My expression fell at the news. "Well, that's a bummer." I waved my hand dismissively. "It's fine. I'll wear a hood or something to cover my face."

"It'll still be suspicious—three people, roughly the same height, two sticks, and one—" Martel paused.

"Hey," I interrupted, giving him a watch-what-you-say-here death glare. "One what?"

"One hourglass," Martel finished succinctly, his gaze flicking around nervously. "You'll be spotted right away."

"Doing nothing is not an option." Frustration edged my voice. "I'll go alone if I have to."

"There is something..." The orc turned on his heel and headed into his shop. We followed him to the shelves where I'd seen the glowing orb. He opened the box next to it, retrieving a small handful of what looked like lapel pins in a variety of colors.

"What are they?" Carver asked, leaning in for a closer look.

"They're glamour buttons," Martel replied as he examined the pins. "They change the wearer's appearance after you recite the incantation."

This was a shop of broken items, making me cautious. "What's wrong with them?"

Martel wiggled his brow. "Nothing, as long as you don't mind being ... less than attractive. I believe every creature is beautiful, but these buttons press the limits of even my grace. The woman who paid to have them crafted didn't specify to the witch that she wanted multiple attractive personas. She asked for the glamour to get her noticed." He chuckled. "The witch did her dirty with these. Still, it was in the letter of the law for the agreement, so she had to pay for them. I took them off her hands for half the price." He smiled. "I was going to fix the glamour to resell, but I put them in this box and forgot about them."

"Does that happen often?" I asked.

Martel mused quietly for a moment, then said, "Yes. I should go through my shelves and drawers sometime and do inventory."

"But you probably won't." I smiled knowingly. Like recognized like. I had so many bins, jars, and baskets around my house full of items I didn't remember. Out of sight, out of mind.

He shook his head and chuckled. "I probably won't."

"No matter," I assured him. "I don't need to be pretty, just unrecognizable. I'll take a pin."

"Same," Carver chimed in, his voice laced with determination.

With a playful glint in her eye, Ryker teased the orc, "Will you still want me if I'm grotesque?"

"Aw, honey," Martel replied with a charming smile. "That's what the light switch is for." He punctuated his words with a wink.

We all burst into laughter, easing some of the tension in the room.

Martel held out the buttons, a mischievous glint in his

eye. "Pick your poison."

"I'll take yellow," I said confidently, scanning the array. "It looks great on my skin tone."

Carver reached for the green button, nodding in approval, while Ryker opted for pink, her choice made with a smirk.

I deftly pinned the button onto my sweatshirt, and my friends followed suit, attaching theirs as well.

"Now what?" I asked eagerly, anticipation lacing my voice. "What's the incantation?"

"Always seen, jellybean," Martel declared with a grin.

"That is so mean," Ryker commented, her tone playful.

I arched a brow at him. "So, we just say it and poof, we look like other people?"

"Pretty much," the orc confirmed, a hint of amusement in his deep voice.

"And what's the incantation to drop the glamour?" Carver asked.

"Damn." Martel sighed dramatically. "I was hoping you wouldn't ask." He gestured with his chin toward Ryker. "This one never sticks around. I was hoping she'd have to come back before she left again."

Ryker playfully went up on her tiptoes and kissed his cheek. "I'll be back, ya big dork," she promised, her words filled with affection. "So, what's down at the end of the flashing colors? The red light. What are we getting ourselves into?"

"All the buildings have colored lights to indicate what's for sale and what services can be provided," Martel explained, his gestures emphasizing the bustling streets outside. "My place is a blue for generalized goods. I trade, buy, and sell magical and non-magical items that need fixing or that I've fixed. I'm a tinker by trade. Yellow is for accommodations, green for food, and red, well, that's the fantasy district. Sex, drugs, and all kinds of kink."

My stomach started to churn at the mention of the fantasy district. "But Zev..."

Carver placed a reassuring hand on my shoulder. "We don't know anything yet."

"And we won't as long as we're standing around here," Ryker interjected, her tone firm. "Let's get to it." With determination, she touched the pin and recited, "Always seen, jellybean."

My eyes widened in horror as Ryker transformed before me. She morphed into a grotesque man with an oozing sore on his bald head, a couple of inches above his ear. Neck rolls swallowed his neck, and his yellow, nasty teeth were turned every which way in his mouth.

I couldn't help but cringe as I instinctively stepped back. "No offense, Ryker, but yuck."

"Your turn," Ryker said, her voice distorted by the transformation and sporting a strange accent. "Get to it."

I exchanged a grimace with Carver, silently debating our next move. "Together?" I suggested.

He nodded, his expression mirroring my unease.

"Always seen, jellybean," we both said in unison.

"Oh my gawd," Ryker exclaimed in shock. "What the actual hell?"

"Is it bad?" I asked, my voice high and airy. I looked down at my hands, which were covered in sores, my nail beds caked in dirt.

"So, so bad," Carver said, his voice nasally. I gasped at his glamour. His new persona was four feet tall and with moldy green skin. His bright yellow teeth added to his sickly appearance.

I turned my hands over and Zev's mark was still there. It was the only part of me that hadn't been covered in the illusion spell. "Uh oh."

"We'll put a bandage over it," Ryker said. I promise no one will pay attention to your hand."

I turned to a window where I could see my reflection and couldn't believe what I saw. My jaundiced skin was mottled with patches of oozing red sores. Jagged spikes protruded from my chin, and reptile scales were on my arms. My brown eyes were now sunken into hollow sockets. "Who hurt this witch?" I spat, the words dripping with venom. "The woman needs serious psychotherapy," I muttered, my growly voice tinged with a mixture of disbelief and horror. "Hell, I'm going to need psychotherapy." I shook my head, the image burning into my mind like a brand. There wasn't enough brain bleach in the world to erase the monster from my brain. "The trauma is real."

The orc had retrieved a plaster bandage large enough

to cover the symbols etched into my skin. "Here you go."

"Thanks," I replied, pressing the bandage against my palm. I was relieved it stayed in place, considering all the open sores. "Perfect."

"Good news," Ryker chimed in. "I don't think anyone is going to recognize us."

"Bad news," Carver added, "I'm not sure anyone is going to let us into their establishments."

"If your money's good, they don't care," Martel quipped. He gave a low whistle as he looked us up and down. "You all are a sexy bunch."

Ryker playfully punched Martel in the chest. "A kiss for luck?" she teased, puckering her lips.

Martel blew a kiss from a safe distance. "Luck," he declared. "The reverse phrase is For all the haters, see you laters. And yes, laters had an s at the end."

Ryker's grin, filled with crooked, gnarly teeth, sent a shiver down my spine. "Anyone who gets in our way better watch out," she proclaimed, rotating her bulbous hips and enjoying her glamour way too much. "They won't see us coming."

"That's the point," I interjected, shaking my head at the absurdity of it all. "Let's hope no one gets in our way."

"Damn straight," Carver's diminutive persona exclaimed as he pumped his tiny green fist in the air with unexpected enthusiasm.

This was either genius or the worst plan in the history of plan-making. "Let's go," I declared, steeling myself for whatever twisted fate awaited us.

Chapter Fifteen

WE KEPT TO THE SHADOWS AS WE FOLLOWED Martel's suggested path to reach the Brownie District. Trash littered the sidewalks, and the stench was real. Mystery gunk dribbled down walls. The street was empty of cars, but we did see a lone tire roll down the street, emitting tiny screams.

"Is that smell coming from us or the streets?" I asked.

"Does it matter?" Ryker asked. "Stink is stink."

True, but I still wanted to smell nice, even if I looked gross.

We'd gone past five of the colored districts and were passing through the second blue, the one immediately before red. There were signs for a bookshop, trendy clothes salon, lockpick service, and shoe store. I guess they didn't mind doing business near the seedier area of the city. Money was money. Ryker had transferred some bitcoin to Martel, and he'd supplied us with a stack of cash, the only thing that spent in the red district.

"We are so disgusting," Carver said. "If I saw me out somewhere, I would run as far as possible in the other direction."

"At least you don't have open sores or pus oozing from your head," Ryker pointed out.

"I'm covered in fungus."

"Let's just find the stupid bear without getting caught," I told them. If we did, I'd kiss the clever witch with the devious mind who'd come up with these uniquely awful glamours. She'd have had to craft each one from top to bottom. That was a lot of imagination brought to life. The witch was an artist—gross but appallingly talented.

We silently wove through the throngs of otherworldly beings, the atmosphere thickened with a potent blend of allure and danger. Every step we took seemed to draw us deeper into a web of intrigue, where every dark corner held a secret and every whispered promise carried a price.

A man staggered out of a place called Potion Puffers. He acted deranged, his laughter echoing off the walls of the narrow street as he danced away. All the businesses lining the street exuded an aura of seedy seduction. They offered pleasure and pain in equal measure.

We passed Nexus Ale, a tavern near the center of the blue district. The heady aromas of exotic spices mingled with smooth notes of jasmine incense almost canceled the creature-funk emanating from our bodies. Men and women of all shapes, sizes, and supernatural races lounged in the shadows, their eyes hungry for whatever vice they would seek in the red district.

But amidst all the flash, dazzle, and depravity, there was no sign of the giant teddy bear with the yellow bow, which meant we hadn't yet found the clue to lead us to Zev. I wouldn't give up—not yet.

Even in their disguises, I could see the worried glances between Carver and Ryker.

"We keep going," I insisted. My palm tingled under the bandage, and I worked hard to keep my nerves from sending me into full pyro-mode. I was certain Shay told his people to look for someone who could shoot flames from her hands, but I wasn't sure what flames would do to the glamour spells.

Only this felt different than the two times I remember "flaming on." A pulsing warmth emanated from the mark, and the further we walked down the street, the stronger it grew. I stopped in my tracks.

"What's wrong?" Carver asked.

"I'm not sure. I need to turn around."

"Why?" Ryker asked. "Did we miss something?"

"It's not that." I rubbed my thumb across the band. "I have this feeling, and I need to see if it pans out."

We turned around and retraced our steps. The further we walked, the colder my palm got. "Let's go back," I instructed, turning again.

Once again, the further down the street we went, the

warmer my marks became. It might've been my imagination or wishful thinking, but I believed Zev's symbol was playing a game of hot and cold with me.

The Mythos Mysteries Theatre loomed ahead, a giant marquis advertising rare oddities never seen and a live show of dancing, singing, and stripping. A long line of customers waited at the box office to purchase tickets. As we approached, the sensation in my hand grew stronger and began to pulsate.

I swallowed the thick saliva at the back of my throat. "There," I said, pointing to the theatre. "In there."

"I trust your gut," Ryker said. "It's been pretty accurate to this point."

"At least it's a direction," Carver added. "If he's not there, we'll keep looking."

As we reached the entrance to The Mythos Mysteries Theatre, a surge of raw energy coursed through me, and it nearly buckled me in half. What the hell? The symbols on my palm buzzed, pulsed, and heated until the pain grew so intense that I had to stop. It was Zev. I felt him in my soul, and he was in pain. So much agony. I squeezed my eyes, and my tears were a cool balm on my fevered cheeks.

"It's a trap," he'd said in the dream. "We are done, you and I. This is over. Do not come." I understood why he'd said those hurtful words. How had he hidden his pain from me until now? My chest squeezed at what I would find when I entered the theater. He was being held

against his will, and I had to figure out a way to release him.

I stumbled forward. Carver took my arm and steadied me until I could regain my composure. "Zev is near." I took a deep breath, centering my thoughts and calming my racing brain. "He's here."

"I'll get us some tickets," Ryker said. "Wait here."

"Marigold," Carver said. "Talk to me."

"My hand. I can feel Zev close. He's…I feel his pain." Tears leaked from my eyes. "What could hurt an ifrit to this degree?"

Ryker returned quickly. "I scalped some tickets off a group that had just gone through the box office," she explained. "I paid them triple to get back in line."

Carver nodded as he put his arm around my waist. "Let's get inside. Whatever is happening to Zev is taking its toll on her through the mark."

The air inside the Mythos Mysteries Theatre was thick with the scent of sweaty creatures, buzzing with anticipation for the show. Pain heightened as we made our way down the ornate corridor.

I only had a sliver of his soul, and I was near passing out. How bad did Zev feel?

The plush red carpet muffled the sound of footsteps as we entered the main auditorium. Much like the hallway at the hunter's place, the vast, cavernous chamber seemed impossibly large. Rows upon rows of red velvet-covered seats stretched out towards the stage. Each seat and row had a number and a letter. Our tickets were for row C, seats 2, 3, and 4. It was close enough to the stage to make my guts twist, but now, the pain in my hand wasn't as extreme.

The velvet had faded in spots, the carpet bore stains, and the place smelled musty and old. What once might have been a haven of grandeur now felt like a den of darkness, a gathering place for the foulest entities imaginable.

"Ladies and gentlemen," an announcer called out. "Please take your seat as we present the Corruption of Adam in the Garden of Eden."

The velvet curtains slid apart. The stage, framed with twisted beams covered in flora with gnarled branches, was lit a sickly shade of green. The twisted misshapen branches hung like skeletal fingers from above, casting long, sinister shadows across the platform.

Snake music began to weave a hypnotic spell as a troupe of half-naked dancers, both male and female, emerged onto the dimly lit stage. Their movements were fluid and sensual, synchronized to the enchanting rhythm of the airy flutes and pulsating drums. With each step, their undulating hips echoed the sinuous motion of serpents. It was mesmerizing.

Amidst the spectacle, a large wooden X was wheeled onto the stage with ominous purpose. Bound to it, a figure emerged, scantily clad and vulnerable, his dark, swarthy complexion unmistakable even in the dim light. A gasp escaped my lips as recognition dawned.

Carver's grip tightened on my hand. "It's Zev," he muttered.

I nodded numbly, transfixed as a slinky woman with long golden hair, the epitome of allure and danger, began a seductive dance around the bound ifrit. Why wasn't he escaping? He wasn't in a container. The bindings had to be some kind of magical shackle. He couldn't get free. My palm itched, but the pain had settled into a dull ache.

With each sinuous movement, the woman's body undulated like a serpent, weaving a mesmerizing spell around him. She approached Zev, her movements fluid and graceful, as her hands trailed over his body with a boldness that spiked rage in my entire being. With each touch, flames from his skin licked at her fingers, dancing in a hypnotic rhythm as if eager to be tamed by her captivating presence.

With a daring smile, the woman took the flames into her hands, swirling them around her with an effortless grace. What in the ever-loving fuck was happening? This didn't look like torture. She twirled and spun, his flames bending and swaying perfectly with her movements.

My breath caught in my throat as the woman produced an ornate ceremonial blade from thin air. Fear coursed through me as she brandished it above her head as she ran to Zev.

"No!" I screamed, but from my monstrous form's mouth, it sounded like a croak.

With a flourish, the woman did the unexpected. She used the blade to free Zev from his bonds, and as he stepped down from the cross, his body ignited in flames like I'd never seen before. The crowd in the theater erupted into cheers and applause.

In another dramatic twist, Zev pulled the woman into his arms, kissing her passionately as she was engulfed in his fire. Their ardent display was met with gasps of delight from the audience. But just when I thought the spectacle couldn't get any worse, the flames extinguished, and the slinky femme fatale was wearing nothing but a pair of red underwear. She turned in Zev's arms, his hand the only thing covering her breasts, and with a mischievous grin, she unleashed a torrent of fire from her mouth over the tops of the audience's heads. As the breathtaking inferno evaporated, the audience went freaking wild.

Me? I was pissed. I didn't believe for one moment that Zev had any choice in that little act. The man didn't love public attention, and he definitely wouldn't be performing for this crowd willingly. But someone was the puppet master, and I would find out who before the final curtain call.

And fire them.

Literally.

Chapter Sixteen

I STOOD UP AND SHOVED MY WAY INTO THE AISLE. My large, oddly shaped body made it hard to navigate. Someone kicked my leg as I passed by and shouted at me. "Sit down, you ugly butt crumb!"

Carver and Ryker were right behind me, and Ryker smacked the shouter in the head. He took one look at her grotesque form and decided he didn't want to insult me anymore.

"Where are we going?" Carver asked as we exited the main chamber into the hallway. "And what the hell was Zev doing up there on stage with that woman? That didn't look like he was caught, at least not unwillingly."

My palm had started to warm again the moment we'd exited into the hallway. I flexed my fingers, confused as to what it all meant. "I don't know what's going on, but that wasn't Zev. Or at least it's not the Zev I know. He wouldn't prance around half-naked on a stage and give a fire show to a bunch of depraved assholes."

Carver grabbed my arm and yanked me to a halt. His gaze met mine. "That's exactly what it looks like he did."

"You look like a walking booger, Carver. Looks are deceiving.," I told him, taking my arm back. Zev had been in pain. I'd felt it.

"What's the plan, Stan?" Ryker asked. "I'd say we go in guns blazing, but I don't have one."

"We follow my hand in an elaborate game of hot and cold," I said. "If Zev doesn't need help, I'll have to hear it from his lips." My brows knitted as I thought about his lips on that woman's. I hated the way she'd touched him and the way his hands had been on her breasts.

If you're not trapped and being forced to act out sexual contact, I thought, *then I will kill you, Zev.*

As we hurried through the labyrinthine corridors of the theater, the warmth in my hand guiding our path, I couldn't shake the feeling of urgency. The narrow passageways seemed to twist and turn endlessly—this freaking place! The walls were adorned with fading posters and vintage sconces of a time past when this place wasn't a cesspit.

"Look," Carver said, pointing to a poster for the musical UnBearable. The poster featured a giant teddy bear with a yellow bow around its neck and sitting in a rocking chair holding a baby doll. "It's the teddy bear."

A surge of exhilaration spurred me on faster. That was the final clue from the dream—more proof that we were on the right track. Up ahead, a door with a sign that read "employees only" was guarded by a menacing behemoth with grayish skin and beady eyes. The man was intimidating. However, the pulsing heat in my hand told me that he was standing between me and my djinn.

Carver, that clever, clever witch, wasted no time in pulling out a vial filled with a strange, blue liquid. "Hold your breath," he commanded, his voice low and urgent, as he gestured for Ryker and me to keep moving.

I obeyed, holding my breath as we hurried toward the thug and the door he guarded. Carver's swift motion was like a blur as he threw the delicate ampule against the wall near the man, and a hiss of gas escaped, enveloping the gray man in a cloud of mist.

The effect was immediate. The guy staggered, clutching at his throat, before collapsing to the ground in an unconscious heap. I threw the door open, and we darted through. I closed it behind us and waited until we were several feet away before I took another breath.

"Wow." I high-fived Carver. "That was awesome. Where did you get the knockout gas?"

"I used a few items from Martel's store and made a couple of them when you were showering," he replied. "I thought we might need some kind of defense, especially the way this trip has been going."

"It was good thinking, Buddy," Ryker patted him on the shoulder. "Now, let's go before you're forced to use another." She looked at me. "Where to next?"

"This is the right way." My hand was on fire again—thankfully, not literally, but it burned like it.

We hurried down a dimly lit hallway, through a crossed corridor, and then through a pair of double doors that led to the stage area. We were right in the middle of a bunch of theater people. Dancers and stagehands were everywhere, and I was surprised that our presence hadn't caused a commotion. We were truly heinous to look at. They barely glanced at us, and in our current form, which was pretty darn suspicious. We kept moving until we reached the back of the theater, the pulsating heat working double time.

Near the dressing rooms, there was a door that displayed "Manager" on a metal plaque mid-top center. I turned the knob. The hallway was empty. That was a relief. Another stick bomb wasn't on my list of favorite things.

"It's locked," I hissed.

Ryker stepped up. "Let me handle it." She retrieved a small leather lockpick case from her pocket. "I also got a few things from Martel."

"Are you any good at—" Before I could finish my question, she deftly opened the door. "Never mind."

This was it. Zev was on the other side of the door. I knew it to my core. You better be in deep-ass trouble, mister.

"There's no one in here," Carver observed.

The room was a curious blend of elegance and chaos, with plush velvet curtains framing the windows and intricately carved wooden furniture scattered about in disarray. A delicate scent of oleander hung in the air. But Carver was right. The room was empty of people.

On the desk, an empty decanter-sized clear glass bottle sat tall amongst the paperwork and files. Its surface was adorned with intricate etchings that reminded me of the cuneiform symbols on my hand. The bottle shimmered as it caught the light.

"Guys," I hissed. "Over here."

With trembling hands, I reached for the container, the warmth in my hand intensifying as I touched the cool glass. Instantly, a vortex of smoke swirled inside the bottle, and Zev's voice echoed through the room.

"I'm here, *libbu ša*. You have found me, but you cannot save me. Go, before you're trapped, too."

Relief flooded through me at the sound of his voice, mingled with a newfound confusion about his unexpected prison. "It's him," I said.

"Where?" Carver asked.

"Didn't you hear him? He said he's here. That he can't escape."

Carver's brow dipped. "I didn't hear anything."

"Neither did I," Ryker concurred.

I grabbed the bottle, and everything changed.

This was the Hunter's tearoom, and I watched a fly on the wall as Zev addressed Shay as if they were old friends. "Thank you," he said to the two-faced not-a-god asshole. "I will send payment soon."

"I trust you," Shay said. I know you're good for it." He

finger-combed his thick, wavy hair. "Did you think about giving Lamia the meeting she requested?"

"It's been over for a long time." Zev's expression darkened. "There is nothing left between us."

Shay laughed. "My man, I don't think she got the memo." He sighed. "Ah well, better days for the three of us. It was good to see you, Za'fir. I hope we meet again."

Zev crossed the room to the carmine door and exited the room. When he walked onto the street, he froze. Literally, as if stone. I felt helpless watching as a woman uncapped a glass decanter and said, "I bind thee, Za'fir, bathed in fire, birthed in ash, enter this bottle that can't be smashed, flame makes it stronger, you are free no longer, mine for eternity as it always has been, as it will always be."

When she finished, Zev's mouth opened, and tendrils of smoke fled through his eyes, nose, mouth, and ears and into the bottle. The woman capped it with a clear lid. She held the bottle to her lips and kissed it gently. "You will obey me, Za'fir, or I will make sure you never leave this bottle again." She gestured to two familiar men, Cooper and his buddy Baldy. "Take the body to the theatre. And if I see even one scratch on his skin or a hair out of place, I will make you pay dearly." She flicked a forked tongue at them, and they both hurried to retrieve Zev's body from where she'd paralyzed him.

Carver took the bottle from me, and the vision faded. I was angry and horrified. "She made Zev her slave." I blinked back tears. "We have to get him out of there."

I quickly explained what I'd seen to Ryker and Carver, including what I could remember of the incantation and the forked tongue at the end. Talk about heebie-jeebies.

"Lamia was the name of a Greek goddess who seduced men and bent them to her will," Ryker informed us. "She would use her poison to paralyze men, then hypnotize them to do her bidding."

"That sounds a lot like what's happening right now." I touched the glass. "Can you hear me?"

"Yes," Zev responded. *"Lamia is dangerous. She was my first and only master. She plans to make it a more permanent position. I will never be free."*

"I don't believe that. I won't let her win."

"Marigold, this is diamond glass. It can't be smashed. It can't be melted. It can't be cut. I tried to escape, and my fire made it stronger. I'll be okay, as long as I know you are safe. Go."

"Not without you."

"This vessel is hers. If you take it, she will find you."

"What's he saying?" Ryker asked.

"That he's a lost cause." I pulled the bandage off my palm. I held up my hand and showed the bottle Zev's mark. "If you didn't want me in the thick of it, then you shouldn't have marked me."

"I'm pretty sure you marked yourself," Carver volunteered.

I glared at him then glared at the bottle. "Well, who cares? I'm marked. I've got a piece of your soul in me.

And now I want all of it...out of this bottle, I mean, and back into your body. Where is your body?"

"Somewhere you'll never find it, thief," a woman said. "I'll take my bottle. If you leave now, I'll let you keep your lives."

It was the bitch who'd trapped him in the bottle, then took his body on stage and ran her hands all over it. "Carver, you got your blue thing handy."

"Yep," he said. "Get ready."

"Ready," Ryker chimed in.

"Sorry, lady, but the djinn's coming with me." I held my breath as Carver threw the knockout potion. However, it didn't knock Lamia unconscious. It did, however, startle her long enough for us to get past her. I'm sure we seemed awfully fast for a group of monsters. We ducked into the dressing room and out of sight. It was time to change. "For all you haters, see your laters," I whispered. Carver and Ryker did the same. "Let's find some less conspicuous clothing." I pointed to a rolling wardrobe rack at the back. "There."

Carver still carried Zev as we ducked behind the wall of costumes.

"I'll take him," I told my friend.

"Are you sure?" Carver's expression was worried.

"Just give me my djinn, Carver." He reluctantly handed me the bottle.

"We need to get out of here," Ryker said. "This place is going to be swarming with rough-and-ready types soon."

"I'm not leaving without Zev's body." I looked at the bottle. "It's the only one you have, right? There are no spares anywhere?"

He chuckled. "Oh, how I have missed you. No, there is no spare."

"That settles it, then. You all can go, but I'm not leaving without his meat suit." I changed into a pale, gauzy dress that hit me below my knees. It was a little tight across the boobs, but otherwise fit okay. Ryker put on some kind of uniform, while Carver dressed in a black hooded Grim Reaper robe. We were totally inconspicuous.

"Is there another robe?" I asked. "I can use it to hide the bottle."

Carver handed one to me, and I slipped it on. "Perfect," I said, then shook my head at the three of us. Ryker looked like a soldier being escorted to her death. "Nope," I reiterated. "Not conspicuous at all."

When we stepped back out into the dressing room, I noticed that the female dancers were chatting while the men were virtual zombies. When I got to a brunette doing her hair and makeup alone, I casually said, "I'm a new dancer. I'm part of the new Death In Paradise number."

"Welcome aboard," she said without even looking at me.

"Thanks, yeah. Uhm. Who was the hottie on stage with Lamia in that first number? He scorched that stage and not just with flames."

That got the dancer's attention. She lowered her voice, "He's her special case," she said. "But don't let her catch you talking about him. That will get you fired on the spot...or worse."

"Noted. Good advice," I said. "So he doesn't use the dressing room with the rest of us peons, huh?"

"Not even," the girl said. "He has his own room, V. I. P. It's across the stage. Here is some more advice: avoid that area like your life depends on it because it does. Two weeks ago, Lamia caught Larissa poking around, and she stabbed her with that big knife she uses in the first act. It's not a prop."

"Thanks," I said, tipping my head to her. I held Zev close to my body under the robes as we exited.

We stuck to the shadows behind the curtain to avoid detection. Carver and Ryker had stopped asking questions and just let me take the lead. It was much easier that way.

"You are very good," the ifrit said. *"You could talk a starving man out of his last piece of bread."*

"But I wouldn't."

"Which is why you are special. You use your power for good."

I snorted a quiet laugh. "If by power you mean bull-shit, then sure." I saw the door the dancer had talked about. "His body's in there," I said to my friends. "Let's get it and go."

"And how are we supposed to carry a body out without getting caught?" Ryker asked.

The questions were back. "I'm a discovery thinker," I told her. "I'll know what to do when the time comes."

"I don't feel reassured," she said sarcastically, but she kept following, so I took it as a win. A surge of triumph rushed through me as we made it to the door. Bonus: it was unlocked!

My victory didn't last. Inside the room, Lamia stood behind Zev's body, a knife pinned against his throat. A slow smile spread across her lips. "Is this what you were looking for?" She nipped the skin just enough to make it bleed. "Give me the bottle, darling. And I'll care for Za'fir as if he were a rare treasure. Because he is. And my ifrit is priceless." She narrowed her stare. "However, if I can't have him…" She cut deeper into his flesh. "No one will."

Chapter Seventeen

IF YOU'RE IN THAT BOTTLE, HOW IS SHE CONTROLLING your body? I asked Zev. I did it in my head, hoping that he still could hear my thoughts. My speech was at warp speed, time was running out fast.

She can project herself into my brain. She only needs my hardwiring and a small amount of my power.

He had been in so much pain when I felt him earlier through the mark. There had to be more to it than simply projecting her mind into his.

"You were in pain," I insisted. *"Earlier. I could feel it."*

"She must extract some of my essence to run my body. When she shoves it inside, I am in control for a moment until she throws me out. The process is unbearably painful."

So, she basically uses you as a power supply before she takes over your personality?"

"Partially. She's a powerful supernatural being."

"And I'm not. I can't take control of your body."

"Nope," he agreed. *"Take the deal. She will keep her word.*

"You both know I can hear you, right?" Lamia said. "I am connected to Zev's spirit through his body."

I met her gaze with raised brows. "I did *not* know that," I said out loud.

"I knew it," Zev said. *"But I don't care. Let me go. I don't belong to you, Lamia. I never did."*

She pressed the tip of the knife deeper into Zev's neck. "Zev is right. I'll keep my word, if you take the bargain. Leave, and you will live."

"I'm not leaving without Zev or his body. Also, keep your fricking hands off his body. And his essence."

Lamia's brows rose. "Arrogant, aren't you? I always get what I want."

"Is that what you call trapping Zev?" I took a step forward. "You knew he wouldn't willingly choose you. So, you forced him."

"Irrelevant," Lamia hissed. She smiled, but the curve of her lips was sharp, like the blade she held against Zev's throat. "Perhaps it is enough for me that you never have him." The snake woman had hijacked Zev's brain, and the only thing keeping him from taking it back was his essence being trapped in the vessel I held.

"Marigold..." Zev warned.

Why that ... that scaly tart! I'd had enough of her

threats. I lifted my palm and aimed it at her. Fire shot out of my hand like a flame thrower.

Lamia's eyes widened, and then she began to laugh as she walked into my blaze. "Your fire can't harm me. I am a desert creature. Fire gives me power."

I closed my fist and shook out the residual flames. "That wasn't for you," I told her.

She peered at me suspiciously. "Then who was it for?"

"Me," Zev said from behind her, surprising her as he snatched her knife.

The snake woman screamed as he shoved the blade deep into the back of her skull. She dropped to the ground and began writhing. "This won't kill her," he said. "But it will buy you time to escape while she molts and reforms."

"How in the world did that work?" Carver asked.

If Lamia could jumpstart his body with his essence, I hoped I could do the same. "I have a piece of Zev's soul inside me. I just tried to give it back."

"Marigold." Zev held his arms out to me.

I closed the distance between us and hung my arm over his shoulder, clinging to his bottle with the other. "I'm not leaving without you. I said it, and I mean it."

He stroked my hair and caressed my cheek. "I can already feel my essence leaving this body," he said. "The three of you will never make it out of here with me."

Ryker spoke up. "It looks like we need to find a loophole then."

Zev pivoted his gaze to her. "And who are you?"

"I am Neetra Wijawa, also known as Ryker, daughter of Ratna Wijawa and Rakistu Sha'a." She put her hand on her hip. "I believe you know my father."

"Rakistu Sha'a," he said with wonder.

"You found a loophole." She nodded. "And we'll find another."

I recited the spell Lamia had used. "She said, I bind thee, bathed in fire, birthed in ash, enter this bottle that can't be smashed, flame makes it stronger, you are free no longer, mine for eternity, as it always has been, as it will always be."

"Wow, that's a powerful incantation," Carver said.

"Hello, Carver," Zev addressed. "It is good to see you."

"You as well."

Lamia's human body started to split, and I could see a massive snake trying to wiggle its way out.

"We need to get this show on the road," I said, making a wrap-it-up gesture. "No stupid ideas here. Just hit me with what comes to mind."

"Ice," Carver said. "Heat makes it stronger. What will cold do to it?"

"Good, good." I dragged Zev to the door. "We should try to get you out of here. We can figure it out." My words trailed off as I watched the life drain from his eyes again. The small spark I'd given him had faded. I held the bottle. "Zev?"

"I'm still here," he said.

I was so tired—too tired to think. It felt like every synapse in my brain was misfiring. "Ice, ice, baby," I hummed. "Ice blocks, ice baths, liquid nitrogen, warts. No, not warts." My connections were going awry. "Back to ice baths. The diamond glass gets stronger with heat. Glass blowers use heat." I'd binge-watched three seasons of *Blown Away*, and an idea struck me. I set the vase on the ground.

"What are you doing?" Zev asked, but I didn't have time to answer. The floor was giving birth to a giant snake. "Carver, I'm going to need you." I hit the bottle with my flames, throwing all my love, my anger, my pain, my feelings of betrayal and loss into the fire that poured from me. I took all of it, and I focused the energy onto Zev's vessel.

"Fire makes it stronger," the eclectic witch said. "Isn't this making it worse?"

The clear glass turned cherry red as it reached temperatures that would melt most glass. I stopped the flames. "I don't need ice," I told him. I only need it hot enough that any water will feel like freezing. Hot glass in cold water, go snap, crackle, pop." I pointed to Zev's vessel. "If you wouldn't mind. Hit it."

Carver closed his eyes and began to chant softly, his voice weaving a spell of ancient power. As he spoke, a shimmering aura enveloped him, and when he opened his eyes again, they had transformed into pools of pure liquid H_2O, reflecting the magical energy swirling around us.

With a flourish of his hands, Carver conjured a ball of water, its surface sparkling with arcane energy. He spun it gracefully, each movement imbued with the fluidity of his newfound power, until it became a swirling vortex of mystical water.

With a focused gaze, he directed the watery sphere towards Zev's vessel, the liquid shimmering and pulsating with magical potency. With a swift motion, he released the ball of water, and it struck the decanter with a resounding splash, sending ripples of magical energy cascading through the air.

I held my breath, anticipation coiling in the pit of my stomach as the water made contact with the vessel.

I held my breath and felt soul-crushing disappointment when nothing happened.

A light snap sounded, then a crackle sounded as the glass weakened, and I held my breath for the satisfying pop. *Pop!* The magic of science. The bottle cracked and split into three pieces, releasing a torrent of smoke that spiraled upwards and entered Zev's body the same way it left, through the holes in his face.

"Hot glass in cold water, go snap, crackle, pop," Ryker repeated my words with a smile.

"It sure does," I said, launching myself at Zev when his body animated. "You're back."

"I'm weak, but yes, thanks to you, I am back." He embraced me back. "We must leave. Lamia will awaken, and in a few days, she will recover her memories; that is when she will seek her revenge."

That sounded really awful. "What if we cut her head off?"

"Then she will grow back two," he replied.

"So no head chopping."

"No," he agreed. "No head chopping."

Ryker had a watch on that beeped. "Hey, we have to go. Now. We have two hours to get down to the Brownie docks. We need to get back to Martel's place. He is our ride to the docks. If we don't make it, the boat won't wait for us."

"Can you poof us out of here?" I asked Zev.

"I'm afraid my power is zapped. I could try, but I don't know how far we'd get."

I slid my hand in his. "We'll make it," I said. "We'll do it together."

We all ran across the stage, aghast to realize the show was still going on. Ten snake dancers were getting hugs from albino pythons. I recognized one as the brunette who'd told me where to find Zev.

"Thank you!" I called back to her as we escaped through the corridor that led back up to the front hallways.

Four familiar faces loomed near the entrance to the theatre.

"Son of a bitch," Ryker hissed. "It's Cooper and his boys."

"We should split up," I said. "It will be less conspicuous. You and Carver go ahead. Zev and I will create a distraction."

"Are you nuts?" Carver asked me incredulously. "I can't run away while you set yourself up as bait for these goons."

"Zev said he can apparate a short distance. If we get in trouble, he can just poof us out of there." I gave Zev a back-me-up-on-this look.

His mouth thinned into a grim line. "I can facilitate an escape if need be," he agreed. "Marigold is right," he said to Carver and Ryker.

I don't know why, but hearing him say I was right made me ridiculously happy. "Okay, you two hide for a minute, and we'll draw them off. We'll meet down at Martel's, and if we don't show, go to the boat. We'll meet you there."

"You better show up," Carver groused.

"We'll show," I promised. I gave him a fast hug then repeated with Ryker. I'd gotten my friends into my mess, and I was going to do everything in my power to get them out. When they were out of sight, I waved at the blue men like a lunatic.

"Hey, Dickheads!" I shouted.

Zev groaned, but it got their attention. Cooper and his buddies took off at a sprint. Well, shit. Zev grabbed my hand, and we ran down the hall back toward the stage. The "Employee Only" door was unmanned, so we went down that way. A giant snake wound its way towards us.

Lamia might not remember who we were, but she sure as hell remembered that we'd pissed her off. Blue Man Group was behind us, and a giant snake goddess was in front of us. It was the proverbial rock or a hard place scenario. With danger closing in from both sides, there was no time for hesitation.

Luckily, we were only buying time for my friends.

"You ready to get out of here?" Zev asked.

The snake was slithering fast, and the storm kelpies were storming. "Oh, absolutely."

He grabbed me in his arms, and in the next blink, we were somewhere else. It was dark but warm. "Where are we?" I whispered.

"I'm not sure, *libbu ša*." He held up his finger, and a flame no bigger than candlelight flickered from the tip. Boxes were on metal shelves surrounding us. "We're in a storage room, maybe?"

"I love it when you call me that." I smiled. "*Libbu ša*."

"It is accurate. You're my heart," he said. He pressed my palm onto his chest. "Without you, I cannot survive."

"I think that's been established," I joked. "Just look at the trouble you got yourself into leaving me the first time around.

His expression darkened. "I didn't leave you, Marigold."

"Could've fooled me," I said gently. "You were gone for seven months, and I never heard a peep from you. That feels a lot like leaving. Look, I know it's not your fault. I mean, now I know. But you made choices for the both of us that we should've been making together."

"I don't understand," he said.

"The hexogenist. Dr. Raines. If you were trying to change to be with me, you should've told me."

His eyes swirled with fire, and yet, he still managed to look abashed. "I'm sorry. I...I didn't want to break your heart again. What I was looking for was an impossible feat."

"You want me." I slid my hand down his chest. "I want you."

He stilled my hand from going further south. "It's more than want, and you know it. The stakes are too high where we're concerned."

"I'm still a creature of fire, and you're..." He stopped talking when I set my hand ablaze.

"I'm a creature of fire now, too."

He pulled me close, his body hard against mine. "I can feel my soul intertwined with yours." His voice was a hoarse rasp, filled with dark promise. "I have never had this kind of connection with anyone. Djinns do not have mates. They don't fall in love. It is the way of our kind to remain unattached." He curled his fingers at the nape of my neck, and his breath against my skin made me shiver with delight. "But with you, it has been and will always be my impossible dream."

"Possible," I told him. "The two of us together. Anything is possible."

The air crackled with tension as our gazes locked, the unspoken desire between us becoming impossible to ignore. As if drawn together by an irresistible force, our lips met. I moaned against his mouth as his hands roamed my body.

"Oh, hell, yes." I slid my hands over his shoulders and locked my hands behind his neck. "I've missed you."

"I..." The door to the room we were in rattled to life. Zev grinned ruefully. "To be continued."

"The minute we're off this island," I told him. "Count on it."

We kissed one more time as Zev blinked us out of the building and onto the street. His face was pale, and the fire in his eyes was barely ablaze. "Are you unwell?"

"I'm weakened, but I am stronger with you. Apparition takes a lot of magic on a good day."

"That's okay. We can make it on foot from here." I took his hand. "Follow me."

We were nearly home free, except for the two angry gods and their goon squad. Whatever. I would worry about them after I got Zev off this rock of misery.

Chapter Eighteen

By the time we got to Martel's, my friends had already left. There was a handwritten note pinned on his door that said, *Gone Fishing, xxoo, R. C. M.* Hah. Since Ryker's initial was first, I assumed the message was her doing. Some of the tension left my gut. I was profoundly relieved to know they'd made it to safety.

We didn't waste a moment. With one last glance around Martel's messy and well-loved shop, I whispered goodbye and hoped I never saw the place again in my lifetime.

Zev knew Natheria better than I did, and with a few shortcuts through buildings, it didn't take too long to get to the Brownie District. The feeling of being followed put a real pep in my step. My knee be damned.

The city's constant darkness had helped us stay undetected in the shadows, but the Brownie territory was distinctly different in that it didn't have any high-rise buildings. The morning sun crested the horizon, bathing the district in pale peach and golden light.

The quick shift from night into day took my breath away.

"It's beautiful," I murmured softly, awestruck as if I'd never seen a sunrise before.

Zev put his arm around my shoulders. "Come. The docks are down this street."

Martel had made brownies sound like badasses who stuck it to the man, but from what I could see, the small fae-folk were adorable. Their hair and skin tones ranged from light brown to a rich chestnut, and they moved about with purpose and energy. Their clothing, however, was rich with a patchwork of colorful fabrics that spoke to a less practical nature.

As we made our way towards the docks, the salty tang of the ocean mingled with the scent of damp wood and fish. Small sailboats and bigger fishing trollers lined the port. The brownies might be small, but I saw them loading and unloading boxes that would break most backs. The wooden planks beneath our feet groaned with each step, as I scanned the area for any sign of our friends.

"There," Zev pointed to a midsized deck boat near the center of the port. Our tall, dark-haired companions stuck out amongst the tiny dockworkers and fishermen.

"Hey," Ryker shouted. Surprise and relief lit up her features as she waved at us. "Hurry. It's time to go."

Carver was helping one of the brownies carry a

heavy-looking chest onto a mid-sized deck boat. "About time," he said as we jogged down to join them. "I thought Ryker was going to chain herself to the steering wheel to keep Captain Dalewood from taking off without you."

"My clients won't wait for me, so I can't wait for you," the brownie captain quipped. "All aboard who's coming aboard." He narrowed his gaze at Zev and me. "That means get your ass on the boat if you want a trip to the mainland."

"Aye, aye, Captain." I gave the brownie a salute as I got on the boat. "How long will it take to get there?" I wanted to get as far from Natheria as possible, and I had no plans on ever coming back.

"About twenty-five minutes if the weather holds." He licked his finger and stuck it in the air. "It'll hold just fine."

The boat was spacious, with deck seating for six people and a small cargo hold below. A small rowboat was strapped to the side. I stared at the heavy chest sitting at the center of the deck. "What's in the box?"

"None ya business," Captain Dalewood answered as the engine roared to life.

I glanced at Carver. "It's heavy," he said. "That's all I know. My back will be feeling it for a couple of days."

Zev leaned back, his face weary. He looked pale, and it worried me. I slipped my hand onto his knee, and he met my gaze. "Are you sure you're doing okay?"

"I'm just tired." He shaded his eyes with the back of

his hand. "It's been too long since I have felt the sun on my skin and breathed fresh air."

He'd been gone for seven months, most of that time spent coiled in a glass bottle. "When we get you home, I am ordering a few days of rest until you get your strength back."

He slipped his arm around my shoulders, and I curled into his side. As the boat motored away, Natheria began to fade, replaced by Isla de Altamura.

"That's some crazy magic," I mused. Until recently, I'd never had an inkling that the supernatural and paranormal world was reality. "How can so much be hidden from humans? Are we really that blind?"

"People see what they want to see," Zev replied. "And when something doesn't fit in the box, they find ways to make it fit."

"Truth." I knew a lot of people who would rather believe lies over facts if the lies aligned with their beliefs. "Why are we like that?"

The corner of his mouth tugged into an amused half-smile. "A question for the ages."

I looked at the captain and did a double-take. The small, dark brownie had turned into a tall, older black man. He wore a white sailor's hat and sported a fluffy white beard and mustache. In other words, he looked every bit the epitome of a grizzled sea captain. It was no wonder most humans were still in the dark.

"Once we make land, I've arranged a ride for you all

into Mazatlán," Captain Dalewood informed us. "From there, you can get a plane ride home."

"I have my own plane," Ryker said. "I'll be taking it back."

"But it's broken." On top of that, I was worried about the cartel. "Wouldn't it be better to come back when you have what you need and there's less heat?"

"Martel got me the part I need, and I'm not waiting. Mystara is my baby. You don't leave your baby behind."

"Stubborn," I muttered.

Carver, who'd been resting with his eyes closed, said, "That's the pot calling the kettle black."

Zev did *not* leap to my defense.

"Fine. I'm stubborn. It's an Everlee family trait."

My response elicited grunts of agreement from both Zev and Carver.

Ryker chuckled.

A wave crashed against the side of the boat, splashing us thoroughly and knocking the boat sideways. So much for smooth sailing.

"What's happening?" I hollered to anyone who could answer.

Carver stood up, his feet shoulder-width apart, as he looked around. "Storm kelpies," he answered, shaking droplets off his hand. "I can feel them in the water."

"Those fucking blue men," Ryker seethed. "They won't give up."

"I got this," the captain announced. "Hold on to your hats."

No one but him had a hat on. Ryker grabbed Carver and pulled him down onto the bench with her as we braced for another incoming wave. Captain Dalewood spun his steering wheel to the left, then back to the right and full throttle ahead. The back of the boat took the brunt of the incoming wave.

"These guys are famous for sinking ships," Ryker shouted as he pointed to another wave breaking from about a hundred feet away. "I don't know what chance we stand in this water coffin!"

"Zev?" I made his name a question.

He gave me a reassuring smile. "I will be fine."

I knew he'd been weakened by captivity, but I hadn't been sure how much until he shook his head. "I've got nothing left. I can't stop them." Guilt punched me. This was my fault. Apparating us twice had cost him so much. I'd volunteered the two of us to act as decoys. I'd just assumed that once he was back in his body, his powers would return to normal. However, I'd rather have a weak Zev than a dead Zev any day of the week.

My jaw dropped as I saw four blue figures riding the next wave, their torsos out of the water and their arms crossed over their wide chests. Cooper and his cronies looked like King Neptune and his army on their way to battle. A seagull, its wings spread as it rode the wind, cried out from above. It was the bird equivalent of "you are so screwed."

Tell me something I didn't know.

When the boat stopped rocking hard, Carver stood up again. He outstretched his arms and began chanting.

The air thickened around us as he called on the waterpower of the sylph. He circled his index fingers counterclockwise and intoned, "Power of water and wind, heed my call. Take them down, make them fall." He clapped his hands then pressed his palms in the direction of the blue wall. I watched as water rose from the ocean in a spiral that took off in the direction of the storm kelpies. The further it got from the boat, the larger it became until the spiral seed became a mega downspout that stretched from the sea to the clouds.

The Blue Man Group tried to apply the brakes, but they were no match for a water tornado. It ripped them from the wave and tossed them so far away that I never saw where they came down. The wave they'd created died instantly.

Stunned silence filled the boat until I jumped up and threw myself at Carver in celebration. "Oh, man. You nailed those jerks! They had no idea that air and water trump water alone."

Ryker had joined our celebration on the deck. She punched Carver in the arm. "And they called you soft. Hah. You showed 'em who's boss! Yeah, baby."

Carver winced and rubbed his shoulder. "I wasn't sure it would work. But since we've gotten here, I've felt more attuned to magic. Even my father's aero-craft. It's in me." His eyes were watery with emotion as he met my gaze. "Can we go home now?"

"Land ho," Captain Dalewood called out. "As soon as we drop anchor, you can get the feck off my ship."

A large helicopter's chopping whir filled the air, its blades kicking up a breeze as it descended toward us. It was army green with a large bay door.

"What now?" Was this someone else stalking us from Natheria? Or was it the drug cartel? Neither was a good option. We'd just gotten rid of one problem: why was fate so unfair? Because it was, I told myself, as the bay door opened. I braced myself for offensive magic or machine guns as the whirlybird swooped down on us.

My heartbeat skipped a dozen beats when I saw my sister Iris waving from an open door. Keir Quinn, Iris's druid fiancé, stood beside her, his presence a reassuring anchor amidst the chaos. And his sister Luanne, the fierce warrior, was expertly piloting the aircraft.

"Woo hooo!" I hugged Zev around the neck. "We're safe," I told him. "It's going to be good. Everything will be all right now."

He nodded and then smiled, but it didn't reach his eyes. I knew he was worried about Lamia, but now that my kickass sister was back home from Ireland, she'd help me dispose of the slippery serpent. Iris had gotten the nickname God Eater for eating a god. Lamia didn't stand a chance.

Zev and my friends were safe. That's all that mattered to me right now. As to the rest, I'd make it up as I went along. It had worked out for me so far.

The helicopter touched down about the same time

that Captain Dalewood booted us from his boat. I noisily kissed his fuzzy cheek, and he grinned. Still, it didn't stop him from warning me, "You're bad luck, lass. Best ye stay ashore."

"You got it," I'd told the crotchety brownie. "Thank you again for the ride."

He gave a cursory salute as he watched us row to the beach. Iris and Keir emerged from the helicopter, their faces grim as they rushed to greet us.

"I was so worried." Iris squeezed the stuffing out of me. Keir helped Zev, Carver, and Ryker into the helicopter.

"How did you find us?" I inquired. "It's like a miracle you're here."

"Not a miracle," she explained. "That text of yours scared the crap out of me, and when I couldn't get ahold of you after, Luanne called a buddy in the C.I.A. to trace your phone. Last night, we found it in a dry bag about two miles down the coast. We've been knocking on cartel doors since then. Those bozos had no idea what kind of shitstorm they were dealing with when they decided they'd rather fight than talk. Tru-craft witch—one. Cartel assholes—zero."

I laughed as I climbed on board and sat next to my djinn. He reached across me and buckled me in, a gesture that made my heart happy. The journey had been long, hard, and dangerous, but I got him back. It made everything we'd been through worth it.

"Can you drop me off at my plane?" Ryker asked Luanne. "It's in a clearing, not that far."

"Sure thing," Lu called back. "Okay, folks. Let's get out of here."

"Do you still have my phone?" I asked my sister.

She nodded. "It was on its last leg, so I turned it off." She reached into a pouch in her jacket and handed it to me.

As the helicopter lifted off from the sandy shore, I let out a huge sigh of relief. Goodbye, Mexico and Natheria.

I hope never saw either of 'em again.

Chapter Nineteen

WE'D DROPPED RYKER OFF AT HER PLANE, AND SHE said she'd come by to check on us next week. Now that we weren't on the run, I had so many questions for Zev. But they could wait. Right now, getting Zev home was, first and foremost, on my checklist.

Luanne made us do a "debrief," and I reminded her that I wasn't one of her soldiers and that I'd debrief when I was good and ready. Good and ready wasn't today. Besides, I was aching for a hot meal and a soft bed. Maybe in combination. Especially if Zev was on the menu.

When Iris finally dropped Zev and me at my house, the kitchen was in the same shambles as when I'd left. Zev's gaze went straight to my stove and cabinets.

"This is..."

"A mess?"

He turned his gaze to mine. "Amazing." His slow blink as he said the word made my heart kick up a notch.

"The explosion wasn't supposed to be part of the spell."

I felt strangely shy. I'd been so focused on getting him back that I never thought about what would happen afterward. Just because I found him didn't mean we were going to pick up where we'd left off. I wasn't even sure if he wanted that. But I hoped he did.

His gaze intensified as he walked over and took my hand, the one with the symbol. "What you have done should be impossible."

"Really?" I couldn't believe someone else hadn't stumbled on this kind of spell before. "If djinns put a piece of their soul in these little tokens they hand out, then it seems likely that someone's done it before."

He shook his head as he traced his fingertip across the triangles. They glowed at his touch. "It's...it's as if this is a key and it has unlocked a door that I've never been able to open."

"What's behind the door?"

Zev licked his lips as flames danced in his pupils. "Everything," he said. "The door opens to all possibilities." He tugged me close, and the heat of his body warmed me to the bone. "It's been too long, *libbu sa*. I've dreamt of holding you in my arms. The dreams are no match for reality."

We'd never made love while he was in his fire era

because no mortal could withstand an ifrit's heat, and I was excited to find out.

"Lamia will come for me," he said. "And from what you've said, the hunter will not rest until he exacts some kind of payment from you. This mark makes you a target for both."

"If they come, we'll make sure they regret it," I told him with more confidence than I felt. I didn't want mortal or immortal enemies, but what was done was done. Looking at Zev, I would make the same choices a thousand times over.

"As you say." His lips, a hint of a smile tugging at the corners, brushed against mine in a sensual, glorious way that made my entire body flush with pleasure. He lifted me up and carried me to my bedroom. When he set me down, I wasted no time getting out of the shift dress I'd procured from the costume rack.

Zev's expression was one of pure lust, and I was here for it. I launched myself at him, and we fell back on the bed. His laughter was all the foreplay I needed. I reached down and began to unbutton his pants, happy to see that he was very happy to see me.

He had other plans.

With strong hands, he flipped me over, his lips leaving a scorching trail of fire along my skin. He hesitated, then asked, "Does it hurt?"

"Nothing hurts when you're here with me," I answered, meaning every single word. This was the first time in seven months that I didn't feel my heart constantly breaking. "I've waited so long for you, Zev. I don't want to wait anymore."

He got up and stripped off his shirt, and *ooo la la*, his body was never disappointing. His pants went next, and let me tell you, whoa, he was impressive to behold. He moved over my body and wrapped me in his arms as he entered me, slow and with so much control. I'd been in his arms like this before, but as he thrust inside me, his rhythmic movements bringing my body to the brink of rapture, there was an intense jolt as his blaze ignited within me. Zev's mouth covered mine as I screamed my orgasm, and fire poured from my lips. He took my flames and swallowed them down until the inferno died down, and I was left trembling and sweating in the aftermath of what I could only describe as existential ecstasy.

As we lay there in the aftermath, I noticed my covers had not fared as well as I had. "We need to invest in some fireproofing."

Zev chuckled for a moment before smoothing the hair back from my face. He stared at me. "Why?" he asked. "Why did you risk so much for me?"

"Don't you know?" I wrapped my arms around him and stared him straight in the eyes so he would really hear the truth. "I love you. I'm in love with you. I should've told you that the day we said goodbye, but I was so scared you couldn't love me back."

His dark gaze intensified. "I'm in love with you, Marigold. You are my heart and my soul. Your joys are my joys, and your burdens are my burdens. We're in this together. And together, there is nothing we can't overcome." He kissed me so sweetly that I thought I would melt. "All my heart," he said. "All my soul. I'm yours."

I bit my lip to stifle a sob. I shook my head, then met Zev's gaze once more. "As I am yours."

AFTER ZEV FELL ASLEEP, I got up to get a cup of tea. Thank heavens I had an electric kettle. I plugged in the kettle and put my phone on the charger while I waited for the water to heat up.

When the screen came alive, I had a slew of messages. Most of them were from Iris, two from Michael, and one from an unknown number, probably spam. Iris's texts were filled with a lot of *Where are you? Why aren't you texting me back? Call me.* Michael had asked where I'd kept my spell books, and the second message read, *Hey, can't find Uncle Ro. His work called because he didn't show up today.*

When I read my final message, the one from the unknown number, my heart sank.

If you want your brother back, meet me in Eureka Springs in two days. Bring only the ifrit, or this won't be a happy ending for either of you. I will text you the location after you arrive.

Rowan's kidnapper had said only to bring Zev. Was this an exchange? I hadn't risked everything to bring him home, only to turn around and lose him again.

But Rowan's life was in danger if I didn't act. The message had been sent yesterday, which meant that tomorrow was D-day. As I sat there, I felt the weight of the ultimatum sink in. Zev came out of the bedroom.

"I will exchange myself for your brother," Zev stated as if there would be no discussion.

I gave him a sharp look. "Are you reading my mind? Can you hear my thoughts now?"

"Not all of them, but the ones that have strong emotion behind them come through more clearly."

"There's got to be a better way than handing you over." Though, I couldn't see it. Rescuing Zev had consequences, and my brother was paying the price.

"Do not make choices for both of us that we should be making together." I heard the slight tease in his tone. I'd said those words to him back on Natheria.

I sighed as he took me in his arms. "You're right."

"I love hearing you say it." He gave me a sly grin.

Rowan's life was at stake, but with Zev by my side, I believed we could do anything. Whoever took my brother had no idea what Zev and I were capable of, and I vowed to do whatever it took to bring Ro home.

I'd face this challenge like I did all challenges—head-on—and I would emerge victorious. My brother's kidnappers better wear flame-retardant clothes because they had no idea the firestorm coming their way.

The End...for now.

. . .

Now that Zev's back, how will absorbing his soul affect Marigold? Can they overcome all the odds to be together? And who kidnapped Rowan?

Find the answers to these questions and more in:

Djinn Bottle Blues
(Destiny of a Middle-aged Witch Book 2)

In my family, danger moves faster than a pixie in heat. I'm Marigold Everlee, a middle-aged eclectic witch with a knack for trouble and a soul that houses a piece of my fiery boyfriend Zev's ifrit spirit.

Talk about a girl on fire. Literally.

Sharing a piece of Zev's soul also gives me access to his fire magic. Oh, yeah, we keep things hot.

After a harrowing rescue mission where I pissed off half the folks in a secret supernatural realm—not to mention a snake goddess who wants Zev all to herself—I knew trouble would find us again.

I just didn't expect it to show up on the same freaking day I brought Zev home. Someone who clearly missed the memo on "leave the people I love alone or get fired from life" has kidnapped my brother Rowan.

What do they want? Zev, of course. My popular fire djinn can't catch a break.

With few options, we enlist the help of Carver, an eclectic witch friend and mentor. Then, we're off to unravel the mystery of Rowan's disappearance. With their help, I'll face this challenge like I do all challenges—head-on.

The kidnappers obviously don't know who they're messing with. And if they harm a hair on my brother's head, I will burn their world to the ground. And stomp on the ashes.

New to the Grimoires Universe? Get **Earth Spells Are Easy** to see how it all began.

As a forty-three-year-old, newly divorced, single mom, I know two things for certain, starting over sucks, and magic isn't real. At least that's what I thought. I mean, starting over really does stink, but when it comes to magic, I have to rethink everything.

I've spent the last year since my ex left me going through the motions. Get up. Work. Care for a grumpy teenager. Cook dinner. Go to bed. Wash. Rinse. Repeat.

Nothing changes... Until it does.

After bidding on a box of old books at an estate auction, I'm experiencing changes.

And I'm not talking about menopause.

My garden gnome Linda has come to life. No, really. Her name is Linda, and she never shuts up. A chonky cat with a few secrets of his own has adopted me. And a gorgeous professor of the occult tells me I'm a witch.

Right now, I'm not sure who's crazier—me, Linda or the hottie professor.

If this is my new reality, it's nature's cruel midlife trick. I'm learning fast that earth spells might be easy, but they aren't cheap. All magic exacts a toll, and if I don't master the elements, the elements will be the death of me.

Literally.

Paranormal Mysteries & Romances

By Renee George

Grimoires of a Middle-aged Witch

Earth Spells Are Easy (Book 1)
Spell On Fire (Book 2)
When the Spells Blows (Book 3)
Spell Over Troubled Water (Book 4)
Ghost in the Spell (Book 5)

Grimoires Universe

Burning Djinn of Fire (Book 1)
Djinn Bottle Blues (Book 2)

Peculiar Mysteries & Romances

You've Got Tail (Book 1)
My Furry Valentine (Book 2)
Thank You For Not Shifting (Book 3)
My Hairy Halloween (Book 4)
In the Midnight Howl (Book 5)

Furred Lines (Book 6)

My Wolfy Wedding (Book 7)

Who Let The Wolves Out? (Book 8)

My Thanksgiving Faux Paw (Book 9)

You Can't Furry Love (Book 10)

Witchin' Impossible Paranormal Mysteries

Witchin' Impossible (Book 1)

Rogue Coven (Book 2)

Familiar Protocol (Booke 3)

Mr & Mrs. Shift (Book 4)

Furred Out (Book 5)

Barkside of the Moon Paranormal Mysteries

Pit Perfect Murder (Book 1)

Murder & The Money Pit (Book 2)

The Pit List Murders (Book 3)

Pit & Miss Murder (Book 4)

The Prune Pit Murder (Book 5)

Two Pits and A Little Murder (Book 6)

Pits and Pieces of Murder (Book 7)

Pittie Party Murder (Book 8)

Nora Black Midlife Psychic Mysteries

Sense & Scent Ability (Book 1)

For Whom the Smell Tolls (Book 2)

War of the Noses (Book 3)

Aroma With A View (Book 4)

Spice and Prejudice (Book 5)

Age of Inno-Scents (Book 6)
Aroma Holiday (Book 7)
The Vapes of Wrath (Book 8)

Hex Drive

Hex Me, Baby, One More Time (Book 1)
Oops, I Hexed It Again (Book 2)
I Want Your Hex (Book 3)
Hex Me With Your Best Shot (Book 4)
Hex Me All Night Long (Book 5)

Praise for Renee George

"Grimoires of a Middle Aged Witch is my new favorite series! I want a gnome named Linda of my own. Trust me. Read the series. You will not regret a single delightfully hilarious and heart-warming moment.

~ *Robyn Peterman, NYT and USA Today Bestselling Author of Good to the Last Death series.*

"I love Renee's books, and recommend any of her series! They catch me right up and keep me turning those pages."

~*Yasmine Galenorn, New York Times Best-selling Author*

"Renee George has crafted a fantastic start to this magical midlife adventure. Pick up Earth Spells Are Easy today! You won't be disappointed."

~*Dakota Cassidy, USA Today Bestselling Author*

"I'm loving the Paranormal Women's Fiction genre! Renee George's humor shines when a woman of a certain age sniffs out the bad guy and saves her bestie. Funny, strong female friendships rule!"

-- Michelle M. Pillow, NYT & USAT Best-selling Author

About the Author

I am a USA Today Bestselling author who writes paranormal mysteries and romances because I love all things whodunit, Otherworldly, and weird. Also, I wish my pittie, the adorable Kona Princess Warrior and my two cats Ash and Simon could talk. Or at least be more like Scooby-Doo and help me unmask villains at the haunted house up the street.

When I'm not writing about mystery-solving were-cougars or the adventures of a hapless psychic living among shapeshifters, I am preyed upon by stray kittens who end up living in my house because I can't say no to those sweet, furry faces. (Someone stop telling them where I live!)

I live in Mid-Missouri with my family and I spend my non-writing time doing really cool stuff...like watching TV and cleaning up dog poop